CANNIBAL TERROR

D___ landed on the bottom in high ___ass. The Indian applied ___ore pressure, his face red from his exertion. Pain lance_ D_vy's arms, and he could feel his rib cage begin to buck'e ___ hairy warrior was tremendously strong, the stro___ Davy had ever gone up against. He wrenched to the ___ ___s shoulders rippling. It had no effect. The hairy brute ___ slowly but surely squeezing the life from him.

Th___ ___e warrior did something even more horrifying. He grin___ ___xposing his front teeth. *They had been filed to shar___ ___ts!*

Da___ ___uld not comprehend why anyone would want to mutila___ ___eir teeth so horribly. As if in answer, the man's head d___ ___d and those pointy teeth sank into his shoulder, biting through the buckskin and into his flesh.

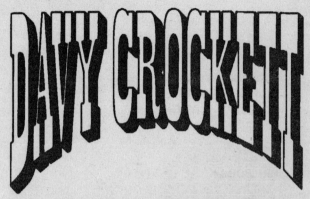

CANNIBAL
COUNTRY

David Thompson

LEISURE BOOKS NEW YORK CITY

To Judy, Joshua, and Shane

A LEISURE BOOK®

October 1998

Published by

Dorchester Publishing Co., Inc.
276 Fifth Avenue
New York, NY 10001

ISBN 0-8439-4443-9

Printed in the United States of America.

CANNIBAL COUNTRY

Chapter One

"Land sakes!" Flavius Harris declared. "Did you hear that?"

Davy Crockett could not help but hear the piercing scream that sliced the humid air like a razor. Reining up, the brawny Irishman scanned the thick vegetation that hemmed them in. His calloused hands closed firmly on Liz, the rifle he had named after his beloved second wife.

The cry was repeated. After rising to a shrill shriek, it faded to a gurgling whine. All other sounds—the chirping of birds, the chattering of squirrels, the throaty croaks of bullfrogs—abruptly died.

Goose bumps broke out all over Flavius. Like his companion, he was dressed in buckskins and moccasins and sported a rifle and a brace of pistols. He licked his thick lips, regarding the rank swampland with outright dread. "Maybe it's one of those three-toed skunk apes the Texicans warned us about," he whispered, afraid the creature would come crashing out of the undergrowth to rip them to shreds.

Davy did not comment. Most folks would scoff at the notion, would brand it as silly. Once, he might have done the same. But since starting his gallivant, he had seen things few living souls had, beasts of legend and lore that by rights should not exist. So he was not about to reject the Texicans' tales offhand. Still, the cry had sounded human, a wail of terror and torment mixed in equal degree. "We should take a look-see."

"Are you addlepated?" Flavius responded. His friend was forever poking their noses into matters better left alone. The result had been calamity after calamity. Flavius would rather ride on as if nothing had happened. "Let's just keep going."

Davy was already dismounting. He let the reins dangle, pulled his coonskin cap lower, and moved toward a break in the thick growth.

"You're leaving your dun here?" Flavius said. It was the height of folly, he thought. How else were they to make a quick escape if one were called for?

"Safer," Davy said. "Too many snakes and gators and such."

Flavius swallowed hard. He did not like to be reminded of the many dangers that lurked on all sides. The vast swamp was home to a host of fierce beasts and poisonous serpents. To say nothing of quicksand, sinkholes, and assorted other menaces. Plenty of reason, in his opinion, to fight shy of it as they would the plague. But when Davy had heard they could shave a full week or better off their trek by cutting through instead of going around, he had led them straight on in.

A Texican acquaintance had told them about the trail they were following—a ribbon of dry, solid ground that wound through the rank marshy wilderness. It was the *only* safe route to take. The man had made it plain that under no circumstances must they stray afield. Yet that was exactly what the Irishman was about to do.

"You can stay here if you want," Davy said. He knew

Flavius as well as he did himself, and he knew that his friend had to be greatly upset.

Crooked trees choked with leaves and vines reared above them, shrouding the trail in gloom. Shadows flickered and writhed at the boundaries of Flavius's vision, and in his mind's eye he imagined enormous shaggy bears and bristling panthers waiting to pounce. "Not on your life," he declared, sliding from the saddle.

"Someone should watch our mounts," Davy said, offering his friend an excuse.

Flavius shook his head, his moon face and balding pate glistening with perspiration. "Where you go, I go." He was not about to let Crockett out of his sight. If they were separated, he would be in dire straits. He made no bones of the fact he wasn't the woodsman his friend was. Without Davy, his chances of making it through the swamp were slim.

"Suit yourself."

A few yards from the trail the ground became soft, spongy. Davy made no more noise than a ghost would as he glided down an incline to the edge of a broad murky pool. There was no telling how deep the water was, or what might be hidden just under the surface, waiting for hapless prey to stray within range of powerful teeth-rimmed jaws. He decided to skirt it, and bore to the right.

Flavius felt his mouth go as dry as a desert. The eerie silence, the tangle of twisted growth, the foreboding pool combined to set his nerves to jangling like Matilda's dinner bell when he was out in the fields plowing. He tried to make as little noise as Davy was doing, but he was not nearly as adept. No one was. Among the frontiersmen of west Tennessee, Crockett was widely regarded as the best marksman and tracker. The last three years in a row, he had won the annual turkey shoot by not missing the mark once.

A faint sound fell on Davy's ears. A sound he could not quite identify. "Do you hear that?" he asked.

9

The only thing Flavius could hear was the hammering of his own heart. Which did not surprise him. Crockett had the eyes of a hawk, the ears of a bobcat.

Davy went faster, placing each foot with care, alert for bogs or quicksand. The region reminded him of the swampland he had explored in Florida during the Creek War. A slithery movement in the water alerted him to a snake. He brought Liz to bear, but the reptile vanished in high reeds.

Flavius was sure they were wasting their time, sure an animal had made the cry. More than likely it was a wrathy painter. Once, in Tennessee, not far from his farm, he'd heard a screech just like it, and later discovered a big cat had been observed prowling the vicinity.

A dank scent tingled Flavius's nostrils. Sort of like the musty odor of rotten logs, although none were to be seen. A mosquito buzzed in circles in front of his eye, and he swatted it away. Soon another took its place, the biggest danged mosquito he had ever seen. Part bird, he reckoned, as it alighted on his leg. He took delight in smacking it, in crushing the nuisance to a pulp. Then he looked up, and winced. He had earned a glare. "Sorry," he apologized.

Davy sighed. His friend was forever making mistakes that might well cost them their lives. He had to remember that Flavius was a farmer first, a woodsman second, whereas *he* was a hunter pure and simple, a backwoodsman born and bred. When anyone asked what he did for a living, that was what he told them.

Since earliest childhood, Davy had loved the woods. Loved them with a passion few appreciated. As a boy he had spent whole days off by his lonesome, seeking game. Fact was, he had skipped school more times than he had shown up, to do just that, and it had gotten him into no end of trouble. He could still feel the sting of his father's switch whenever he recalled the tannings in the woodshed.

A strip of muddy earth drew Davy's interest. A fresh print

stood out like the proverbial sore thumb. Going over, he sank onto a knee.

Flavius joined him, his eyes widening. "Well, I'll be," he marveled. "That beats everything all hollow."

Davy had to agree. The print had been made by someone traveling through the swamp in their *bare feet*. No one, not even the few Indians who dwelled there, would be so foolhardy. Probing in the grass that bordered the mud, he found another track. The distance between the two and their depth told him the man had been running. Recklessly so, since the tracks led into a small bog and out the other side. Davy went around.

Flavius wiped his palms on his buckskins, one after the other. Vividly, he recollected tales the Texicans had related of an especially savage tribe that inhabited the marshy wilderness. His scalp prickled.

Davy vaulted a log, climbed a low knoll. The footprints led up and over. Beyond lay a morass of dark pools, impenetrable thickets, and stooped trees. He was about to start down when the faint sound was repeated. This time he recognized it, and he broke into a run.

Flavius stayed glued to his friend's heels. Under no circumstances whatsoever was he letting Crockett out of his sight. They were at the bottom of the knoll when Davy heard a soft whimper from directly ahead.

A grassy tract framed a shallow gully. Davy never broke stride. Leaping across, he was in midair before he saw the prone figure sprawled at the bottom. Like a cat, he spun even as he landed, bringing Liz to bear. But there was no need.

Flavius had drawn up short at the gully's edge. He had been expecting to stumble on Indians, or maybe to find a white man who had gotten lost. So he was all the more startled to see that the maker of the tracks was neither. "Dog my cats! It's a Negro!"

Davy Crockett absently nodded. He'd seldom had any personal dealings with blacks. They were fairly common on many of the larger estates, used mostly as field hands. Slaves, imported from distant Africa, and elsewhere. No one in his family had ever owned any, and he did not think much of the practice.

During the Creek War Davy had met a pair of blacks while on a scouting mission. They had been brothers, captured by the Creeks and badly abused. Stealing a pair of Indian ponies, they had escaped. Both had been large and likeable, friendly fellows whose company Davy had immensely enjoyed. They had proven to be of important value since both were as fluent in the Creek tongue as they were in English.

This man was nothing like those two. Except for a strange loincloth, he did not have on a stitch of clothing. Mud caked his legs from the knees down. The rest of his body bore countless scratches and scrapes. His eyes were closed, the eyelids quivering. His lips trembled. Every few seconds his whole body quaked, as if in the grip of a chill. His hands were clasped to his left thigh.

"What's wrong with him?" Flavius whispered. He could not say exactly why he kept his voice low.

"Let's find out." Davy hopped into the gully. The black man did not stir, and Davy hunkered down. The man was strongly built, solid muscle and sinew. It was apparent from the mud and the sweat that he had covered a considerable distance, but Davy doubted exhaustion had brought him low. Reaching out, Davy touched the man's shoulder.

The man's eyes snapped open, rife with blatant fear. He began to sit up, but lacked the vigor. Blinking wildly, he looked at the Irishman, then at Flavius. His brow knit. He spoke a few words.

"What language was that?" Flavius asked.

"My ears for a heel tap if I know," Davy responded. It wasn't any he had ever heard. Bending, he noticed the man's

12

earlobe had been pierced by a thin piece of bone, evidently as an ornament.

Flavius was more ·interested in the loincloth. It had been fashioned from the hide of an animal. That much was obvious. "What sort of critter has spots like these?" he wondered, pointing at one.

Davy had no idea. Smiling, he said, "Don't be afeared. We're not going to harm you." He paused. "What's your name? And what the devil are you doing out here in the middle of nowhere?"

The man frowned.

"Do you reckon he doesn't know our lingo?" Flavius offered.

Davy tried the sign language taught him by the Sioux, but the black man gazed blankly at his flowing fingers. Suddenly a violent tremor struck the man. Alarmed, Davy pressed a palm to his forehead to check for fever. The tremor did not last long, and when it ended, the black's breathing was labored, his chest expanding and contracting with each breath. "What's wrong with you?"

As if the fellow comprehended, he moved his hands aside.

"Oh, Lord!" Flavius breathed.

Two puncture marks low on the thigh explained the man's condition. Davy leaned closer. The fangs had penetrated deep, lancing into a vein. He whipped out his knife, prepared to do what he could, but the black feebly lifted an arm to keep him from trying, and uttered a few more words in the unknown tongue.

Flavius fidgeted. "What's he saying?"

"I think he's telling us it's too late, he's too far gone," was Davy's hunch. And he would have to agree. The flesh around the punctures was discolored, the leg starting to swell. The man had been bitten quite some time ago. How he had kept going with venom pulsing through his body was a mystery.

"What kind of snake did it?"

Davy sighed. Sometimes his friend could be downright silly. How was he to know? The swamp crawled with cottonmouths, copperheads, rattlesnakes, massasaugas, and coral snakes. A single bite from any could prove fatal, although copperhead bites were not as generally deadly as the others.

Rustling in nearby weeds made Flavius jump. Pivoting, he trained his rifle, but nothing appeared. "What was that?"

It could have been anything. Davy started to rise, but just then the black man's eyelids fluttered again and the man groaned loudly. Davy gripped his hand. "This jasper isn't long for this world."

The man sucked in a deep breath, then commenced to sing. Or rather, to chant in a singsong manner, forcing his vocal chords to do his bidding with visible effort.

"What's he doing?" Flavius said, astounded.

"It's his death song, would be my guess," Davy speculated. During his stay with the Sioux he had learned they sometimes did the same. The man faltered, growing weaker by the moment, but gamely persevered.

"Pretty, ain't it?" Flavius wished they could understand. He had an inkling the song was about the man's life, about brave deeds done, about loved ones and whatever else mattered most.

Giving Liz to Flavius, Davy slid an arm under the man's shoulders and lifted to prop him against the bank. His hand happened to brush the man's back, rubbing against what felt like hard welts. Tilting his neck, he saw they were not welts at all, but *scars*. Scores and scores of them. Scars that could only have been made by a whip. Old ones, and some not so old. "Take a gander."

Flavius felt his stomach flip-flop. Unbidden, he recollected the time as a child when his father took him to visit an uncle in Georgia. Along the way they had passed a plantation. Flavius had never seen so much cotton. Nor so many Negroes.

Most had been stooped over, toiling hard under a blazing summer sun. Now that he thought about it, he remembered they had been singing. Although what they'd had to sing about had eluded him.

As the wagon rattled past, a white man on a white stallion had galloped in among the workers to where one stood idle. The man on the stallion had angrily addressed the worker. When the slave did not reply, the man on the horse had struck him again and again, with a whip.

It had been awful. His father had told him not to look, but Flavius couldn't help himself. He'd been amazed the black made no attempt to defend himself. Equally amazed that no one came to the poor man's aid. Outraged, he had exclaimed, "Why doesn't someone do something, Pa?"

"What can they do? They're slaves," his father had said.

"So?"

"The overseer has the power of life and death over them, Son. Granted to him by law. He could shoot every last one, if he were so inclined, and never be held to account."

"That's not right."

"It's life."

Not quite sure what that had to do with anything, Flavius had said, "If someone tried to beat me, wouldn't you stop them?"

"You're mixing apples and oranges. We're freeborn American citizens. Those Negroes are slaves. There's a big difference." His father had clucked to the team. "Besides, the owner of that plantation is one of the richest men in Georgia."

Even more mystified, Flavius had said, "Having a lot of money doesn't give anyone the right to hurt people."

"The rich have always been able to do as they pleased, son. Read the Bible. Or books about the old Greeks and Romans. Since the dawn of time, the wealthy have lorded it over the rest of us. It's just the way things are."

A moan brought an end to the recollection. Flavius saw the black man's spine arch, heard him gasp. Froth bubbled over his lower lip. The end was near. Flavius turned away, unwilling to witness it, and was startled to glimpse a pair of dark eyes peering at him from undergrowth to the west. At least, so it seemed, for when he blinked and shifted, the eyes were gone.

Davy held on as the man convulsed and fingernails dug into his skin. "I'm sorry for you," he said, even though the man would not understand. Once he had been stricken by a mysterious malady while on a hunt, and friends had left him to die. So he knew what it was like to be all alone, far from home and family, at the brink of death's door. "Terribly sorry."

For a few seconds the man stopped quaking. His eyes cleared. They locked on Davy's, and the corners of his mouth quirked upward. Then, like a candle being snuffed, the flame of life in them died. The muscular frame deflated like an empty pouch. The black's hand went limp, plopping to the ground at Davy's feet.

"I thought I saw someone," Flavius said.

Davy carefully laid the body down, and rose. A survey of the swamp revealed no threats, and he was about to bend down to fold the dead man's arms when a familiar sensation made him go rigid. It was an odd tingling at the nape of his neck, just such a tingling as he sometimes felt when unseen eyes were on him.

Others might scoff, might claim it was his imagination getting the better of him. But they had not lived the kind of life he had. They had not needed to depend on their instincts day in and day out merely to survive. They had not honed their senses to a sword's fine edge. They had not learned the hard way that those who ignored their intuition often paid for their neglect with their lives.

Davy had a tough choice to make. Should they take the

time to bury the man? Or get out of there while they could? He did not want to leave the corpse for scavengers to find, but a hint of motion to the north spurred him into snatching Liz and quickly clambering from the gully. "Stay close," he advised, dashing toward the knoll.

"Are we in trouble?" Flavius asked, and knew they were when the Irishman did not answer. Scared that at any instant arrows or lances would flash out of the brush and transfix them, he cast right and left for evidence of hostiles.

At the top Davy halted and crouched. The knoll was only twelve feet high, but it gave him a better view of the surrounding growth. Not so much as a leaf stirred. He probed the depths of the thickets, the shadowy trunks. And in one of the latter, in a fork halfway up, he distinguished the outline of a shape that was not part of the bole but was trying to give the impression it was. "We're being stalked," he whispered.

Flavius fingered the trigger of his rifle, Matilda, and yearned to be safely back in Tennessee. He had lost track of the number of times his life had been in peril since their gallivant began. Oh, for the good old days, when his biggest worry was whether to take a nap after supper or to sit in the rocking chair on the front porch and admire the sunset! If no one were to shoot at him ever again, or try to thrust a knife into his heart, or rip his throat out, or snap his neck, he'd be the happiest gent alive!

Davy slowly swiveled. Another squat form in a patch of weeds and a foot poking from behind a log confirmed the worst. "We have to make a run for it."

"How many do you think there are?"

"Enough."

"I'm ready when you are," Flavius said, when in reality he was not ready at all. He would rather curl into a big ball and pray the warriors went away. Hurting other people, even enemies, did not come easily. As a boy he had been the same. When bullies picked on him, he had always tried mightily to turn the other cheek. Some kids poked fun, accused him of being yellow. But they were mistaken. He simply did not like to see anyone suffer.

"Stay low," Davy said. Heeding his own command, he tucked at the waist and flew from the knoll. At the pool he bore to the left, hugging the shore where less vegetation lent greater speed. No war whoops rent the air. No figures bristling with weapons rose up to bar their path. Could it be, he mused, that the Indians were friendly? That they were not the tribe the Texans had warned them about?

Flavius was hoping the same thing. With his gut balled into a knot, he swung from side to side, his thumb curled around Matilda's hammer.

They had gone less than fifteen feet when a strident yip to their rear brought Davy to a stop. It had arisen from the other side of the knoll. From the gully. He heard splashing, then another yip. Instantly reversing direction, he declared, "I'm going back." And was off like a shot, retracing their steps.

Stunned, Flavius hesitated, then imitated his friend's example. "Why?" It was pure insanity. If he didn't know better, he would swear the heat and humidity were affecting the Irishman's brain. "What's back there?"

That was what Davy intended to find out. The yip had not been a war cry. More like a signal, or a token of triumph. He had a hunch the Indians had done something with the body, and curiosity compelled him to find out what. Yes, he was being rash, but so far the warriors had left them alone. Maybe their luck would hold out a while longer.

The shape in the tree was gone. So was the figure in the weeds and the foot by the log. Davy halted the moment he saw the gully. The black man was propped right where they had left him, with one very important difference.

"My God!" Flavius exclaimed. "They've cut open his chest! What on earth for?"

"His heart."

"Huh?"

"They carved his heart out of his chest," Davy elaborated, Exactly as some hunters were partial to doing with deer. They liked to slice it up raw, or roast it on the spot, and partake while it was fresh.

Insight replaced confusion, and Flavius trembled, much as the black man had done earlier. "Then the tales are true," he said, aghast, horrified that his prospects of ever sitting in that rocking chair again had dwindled drastically. It took every ounce of self-control he had to keep from bolting in mortal panic.

"That's not all they did," Davy said.

Flavius looked again. The black man's eyes were gone, gouged out by a knife and left lying between his legs. Bitter bile rose in Flavius's throat, and he swayed as if drunk. Mutilation was a common practice, committed by Indians and whites alike. Not a practice he condoned. Nor one he cared to have happen to *him*. "Why are we still standing here?"

Without another word Davy rotated on the ball of his foot and departed, holding to a brisk pace but not fleeing pell-mell. Indians valued courage, despised cowardice. Should he show he was afraid, it might provoke an attack. He hoped his partner realized that.

Flavius Harris could not have gone any faster if his life depended on it. His legs were mush, his stomach roiling soup, his mind awhirl with gory images of his own butchered body and of a prancing warrior waving his dripping heart overhead. Stumbling in a rut, he nearly pitched onto his face.

Davy slowed. "Careful. We have to show real grit, or it will be root hog or die," he cautioned.

"I'm fine," Flavius lied.

Once on the south side of the pool, Davy made a beeline through the woods. The absence of the warriors perplexed him. The Indians were out there. He was sure. Yet no one tried to stop them. No outcries were raised. No barbed shafts were unleashed. Maybe, he reasoned, the Indians had only been interested in the black man.

They reached the incline. Rather than risk an arrow between the shoulder blades, Davy backpedaled up it. At the crest he delayed long enough to cover Flavius, then pivoted to sprint to the horses. And at last he understood why the warriors had not bothered to interfere, why the two of them had been allowed to gain the trail unmolested.

Their mounts were gone.

Chapter Two

Some men would have cussed a blue streak. Some would have ranted and raved and stomped their feet and uttered threats against the culprits. Others would have collapsed in despair, sure doom was about to claim them, and given up without lifting a finger to save themselves.

Not Davy Crockett. He did none of that. From earliest childhood his parents had taught him to face life's problems head-on. To adapt to situations as they arose. To see what needed to be done, and do it. The family motto bore that out: "Always be sure you are right, then go ahead."

So now, in the seconds after Davy found the horses gone, he scoured the ground and spied footprints that had not been there before. Prints of moccasin-clad feet, moccasins unlike any he had seen before.

No two kinds were alike. The Sioux, for instance, made theirs differently from the Comanches. These new tracks showed moccasins wider at the toes than at the heels. One set, in particularly soft soil, bore evidence of crisscrossed stitching to reinforce the sole.

Flavius Harris was horrified. Without mounts, it would take them three times as long to cross the great swamp. If they made it. Gone too were the gracious gifts of their Texican friends—their saddles, blankets, and supplies. "What will we do?"

"Get out of here," Davy said, and did just that, briskly jogging eastward along the trail.

Flavius did likewise. After a bit he collected his wits enough to say, "Hold on, pard. Shouldn't we go after the horses? I bet you can track them down with no problem."

"I could," Davy admitted.

"Then why don't we?"

"Because there are eight or nine warriors and only two of us," Davy said. It was a conservative estimate. Probably, there were more. And for all he knew, their village was nearby. Before long, the area might be crawling with scores of painted warriors out for their hides. "The smart thing is to put as much distance behind us as we can before the sun goes down." Few tribes fought at night. The Indians might make camp. That would buy him and Flavius a ten-hour lead, possibly longer.

"Whatever you think is best," Flavius said. But given his druthers, he would rather do anything on earth than *run*. His short, thick legs were not built for it. His big belly, as his wife was so fond of pointing out, was "just so much extra weight" that put an added strain on his limbs and lungs. He was panting heavily before they had covered five hundred yards.

Davy kept glancing back for signs of pursuit. He was encouraged when none materialized, but he could not believe the Indians would allow them to escape unscathed. His hunch was confirmed when, presently, the crack of a twig betrayed a vague form flitting through the undergrowth to the right.

The Indians were *paralleling* the trail, not following it. Biding their time, no doubt, until the lay of the land was in their favor, until they could attack with little fear of being shot. Davy ran faster.

Flavius began to huff and puff like an overheated steam engine. His legs hurt and his chest hurt and his temples were pounding, but he forced himself to go on, spurred by the sharp crack of that twig. He knew what it portended. And he did not want to die.

Time passed. A mile fell behind them. Flavius had an ache in his side, a pang so bad that he yearned to stop and rest. Gritting his teeth, he continued to jog at the Irishman's elbow. Never let it be said he did not hold his own when the need arose.

Davy was aware of the toll their exertion was taking on his friend. Back home in the emerald hills of Tennessee dwelled folks who were inclined to look down their noses at Flavius. Who rated him as no-account because he was not partial to hard work and much too partial to food. Most liked to poke fun at him, and called him a "two-legged whale" behind his back.

Which was not entirely true. Flavius was a trifle overweight, but he could still beat many a backwoodsman at wrestling. And once, when a storm had blown a tree over on a family in a carriage, he had astounded onlookers by lifting the end of the tree all by his lonesome so others could pull a stricken boy out.

Davy felt that Flavius had more real grit than most ten men, and had every confidence his friend would stick with him through thick and thin.

The trail commenced to climb. Briefly, it left the swampland, winding up into a cluster of low hills sprinkled with trees and random weeds. Davy was glad. On the crown of the foremost hill, he stopped so Flavius could catch his breath, saying, "We're safe for the moment. They won't rush us here. It's too open."

Nodding, Flavius bent, his hands on his knees. His buckskins were drenched, sticking to him like a second skin. "Maybe we should dally a spell," he suggested. "Maybe they'll get tired of waiting for us to move on, and leave."

"Wishful thinking," was Davy's response. Warriors on an enemy's trail were like bloodhounds on the fresh scent of a coon. The Indians would not give up until he and Flavius were dead.

Davy prowled the crown. For as far as the eye could see, the swamp stretched in all directions. Many miles to the west lay the fertile plains of Texas, where they had parted with their Texican companions a few days ago. Not quite as many leagues to the south was the Gulf of Mexico. To the east, eventually, the mighty Mississippi River, and New Orleans.

Little was known about the lowland that bordered the Gulf. Settlers avoided it. A few hardy frontiersmen penetrated its fringes, mainly to trap and hunt. But the dark heart that pulsed like a mammoth green monster was as mysterious as the dawn of antiquity. Dozens of souls had disappeared trying to cross, leaving no trace, no clue to the cause.

Some claimed the swamp was haunted. Some believed specters and demons roved the remote bayous. A man in San Antonio had said, in all seriousness, that foul fiends straight from the vilest pits of Hell came out to prowl when the moon was full, and the sound of their howls would chill a man's blood to ice.

Davy had never been the superstitious sort. The disappearances he blamed on hostile Indians. The howling, on wolves. The worst thing to fear in the swamp was fear itself. If a man did not lose his head, he would not lose his life.

Flavius shuffled to a log and sat. Opening his possibles bag, he rummaged inside. In addition to his flint and steel and other personal effects, he had two pieces of jerked venison and some pemmican. That was it. Hardly enough food to last a day. He started to pull out the pemmican, but changed him mind. So what if his stomach was growling like that of a bear fresh out of hibernation? He must ration what little he had, make it last as long as he could.

Davy came over and hunkered down. "How are you holding up?"

"It's great exercise," Flavius quipped. "I keep on at this rate, I'll be skin and bones by the time we get home. Matilda will have a fit. She'll have to alter all my clothes." He brightened. "Or fatten me up." His wife was one of the best cooks alive, her pies having won numerous prizes at baking contests and socials. Thinking about her delicious apple and cherry masterpieces made his mouth water.

Davy dipped a hand into his leather pouch and produced a strip of jerky, which he tore in half. "Here." He gave Flavius a piece, then took a bite.

"You have enough to spare?"

"Plenty." Actually, Davy only had a small chunk left. But he had every confidence in his ability as a hunter. They would live off the land, killing game as needed. It was nothing new. He had hunted most of his life.

Almost as soon as Davy had been old enough to wear britches, his pa had shoved a squirrel rifle into his hands and told him to go fetch meat for the supper pot. That first day it had been a rabbit. And every day thereafter he had brought in something. Never once had he let his family down. It had gotten so his parents and brothers and sisters came to take it for granted. They bragged on him, telling all and sundry that he was the best hunter in four states.

And he was.

Once, some city-bred dandies had come out to the country for some "sport," as they'd called it. They had hired some of the local men as guides and gone off into the brush to hunt. Davy, in his teens, had tagged along as a camp helper.

It had been a real education. The city men had spread out in a line, then had the locals drive game toward them by banging pots and hollering and generally raising a tremendous racket. When the frightened deer and whatnot burst from hiding, the city men had unleashed volley after volley, killing everything that moved, killing much more than they could ever eat. Afterward, they had clapped one another on the back and laughed and praised their ability as fine hunters.

Hunters! But that had not been hunting. That had been slaughter, plain and simple. Hunting, true hunting, was as different from that outright butchery as night was from day. Hunting was a noble profession, as old as the human race itself. Hunting was a test of skill, of wilderness savvy, of cunning and endurance. Hunting pitted a man against Nature for the highest stakes of all: his life, and the lives of those who would starve were it not for his prowess.

In olden times hunters had been respected. Admired. Given seats of honor at council fires, at kings' tables.

A hunter did not do as those city dwellers had done. A hunter did not get tipsy on too much ale and then go out and kill anything that struck his fancy.

A true hunter stalked his prey. A hunter had to know his quarry's habits, had to know where each animal could be found at different times during the day. A hunter had to learn what each liked to eat and where to find the food. Had to know when wild creatures went for water. Where they liked to lay low. Their mating seasons. What their tracks and their droppings looked like. In short, everything.

Hunting was a craft. An art. A family tradition. In olden days fathers passed on their hard-earned knowledge to their sons, who would pass it on to their sons, and so on and so on. Back then, every community, every clan, every tribe, counted on its hunters to flourish, to prosper. They could no more survive without hunters than they could without the spark of life itself.

Hunters were still valued nowadays, but not as widely. More and more people were moving into towns and cities, where most of their needs were met for them. Food could be easily had at any tavern or inn or other public eating place. To obtain fresh meat, all a person had to do was visit a butcher. Survival was simple. What use was a hunter in a land of milk and honey?

Thankfully, out in the country, in rural areas where folks still lived day to day making do as best they were able, hunters were still needed. Still essential. Still respected and honored.

Davy was a young man, but already he had won fame as a coon and bear hunter. Those who did not know a lick about hunting, those who would not know a rabbit track from a oppossum's, marveled at his knack. They thought he had a special gift, that the Almighty had seen fit to bestow extra ability on him. How silly. They did not realize his "knack" was the result of years of hard study and effort.

As his grandma used to say, "Whatever a person puts into a task is what they will get out of it." He had been fifteen before he fully understood her meaning. The same with other sayings of hers, such as: "The world doesn't owe anybody a living." Or:"A little sweat goes a long ways." "Feet of clay get stuck in the mud." And one of Davy's favorites: "Love thy enemies, but keep your gun well oiled."

Just then Flavius asked, "What are you thinking about?" He was puzzled by the distant look that had drifted into his friend's eyes. It was hardly the right time or place to daydream.

"Nothing much." Chewing on jerky, Davy moved to the west slope. If the Indians were down there—and he was sure they were—they were well hidden. In four hours or so the sun would set. Under cover of darkness it might be possible to slip away. All the two of them had to do was stay alive until then.

"Any brainstorms?" Flavius hopefully asked. Over the past several months they had been in a number of tight situations, and in most cases the Irishman had come up with a clever idea to bail them out.

"No," Davy said bluntly.

"Well, I reckon we're safe enough for the time being." Flavius grinned. "They haven't tried to kill us yet."

As if to prove him wrong, the air sizzled to the hum of a streaking shaft. A barb-tipped arrow thudded into the earth within a hand's-width of Flavius's leg. Yelping, he leaped up off the log and tried to jump over it backward. His left foot snagged on the stub of a busted limb, and down he crashed. Which was just as well. For another arrow thumped into the very spot he had vacated.

Whirling, Davy brought Liz up. The shafts had come from the southwest. Racing to the rim, he saw a pair of husky figures melt into the vegetation. He was strongly tempted to shoot, but he held his fire. It might be just what the warriors wanted. To trick him and Flavius into emptying their guns, thus enabling the war party to rush them.

Flavius scrambled to his feet. That had been much to close for comfort! It occurred to him that if the Indians started firing arrows at random at the hilltop, sooner or later one was bound to score. "We should light a shuck," he advised.

Davy had no argument. "Lead the way." He watched their backs as they fled down the opposite side, around another hill, and up onto a shelf overgrown with high grass. "Stop," he directed.

"What for? We haven't nearly gone far enough."

"Lay low." Dropping onto his belly, Davy fixed a bead on a point where the trail circled the second hill, exactly where Indians should appear if the warriors were dogging their steps. Cocking Liz, he tucked the stock against his shoulder.

Every instinct that Flavius had grated against staying put.

There was no way to determine how many they were up against. They courted disaster by lying there while the warriors closed in. The Indians might outflank them, cut them off. "I don't think much of this," he commented just as one of their pursuers appeared.

The Indian had his nose to the trail. Broad at the middle as well as at the shoulders, he wore a simple loincloth and low moccasins. His bronzed body had been painted lavishly, on the face, the chest, the back and arms. He carried a short bow in one hand, half-a-dozen arrows in the other. A knife hung at his hip. No feathers adorned his mane of raven hair, as was customary among some of the Plains tribes.

Davy sighted on the man's sternum. In the tracker's wake filed others, six, seven, eight more. Some were armed with bows, some with lances, others with war clubs. One held a long, slender length of cane whose purpose eluded Davy. He saw neither hide nor hair of the horses, which he took as a sign the animals were being ushered to the village, where more warriors would be called on to take part in the chase.

Flavius couldn't understand why the Irishman didn't shoot before the war party got too close. In the hands of a master archer, a bow was every bit as deadly as a rifle. Even more so, since a bowman could unleash arrows twice as fast as a rifleman could reload and fire. He centered Matilda on the second warrior.

Davy tensed when one of the Indians gazed toward the shelf, but the man did not spot them. Resting his finger on the trigger, Davy curled his thumb around the hammer and pulled it back. It went against his grain to shoot anyone from ambush. But he had to do something to delay the war party.

Even so, at the last instant Davy elevated the barrel a smidgen. Just enough so the bead was fixed on the warrior's shoulder and not on the heart. No more than fifty yards separated them when he smoothly stroked his finger. Liz boomed and bucked, spewing lead and smoke. The ball hit true, spinning the tracker in his tracks and felling him where he stood. Davy grabbed at a pistol to get off another shot, but he was not nearly quick enough.

The rest of the warriors vanished. It was as if the ground yawned wide and swallowed them whole. One second they were there; the next the trail was empty save for the tracker, who was on his side, clutching the wound and struggling to rise.

Flavius tugged at his friend's leg. Having fought Indians more frequently than any sane man would ever want to, he had been taught by bitter experience what to expect. "We have to hightail it."

Davy thought the same. Pushing onto his knees, he turned, and as he did a glittering arrow streaked out of the blue and bit into the ground beside him. The wreath of gun smoke had given him away. Flinging himself across the shelf, he raced for the top. War whoops erupted, punctuated by more shafts.

Flavius did not bother to use his rifle. He had no inkling where the warriors were, for one thing. And he was not a good enough shot to hit a target while on the fly, for another. Not without a heavy dollop of pure luck. So he fled for dear life, his heart hammering each time an arrow narrowly missed catapulting him into eternity.

Davy unlimbered a pistol. At the summit he paused to see if the warriors would expose themselves, but none did.

"Come on!" Flavius urged. Fright lent wings to his flight, and he did not slow again until they had gone half a mile. By then they were on the summit of the last of the hills. Below them unfolded more shadowy swampland overhung by creepers and stooped trees. In a pool to the north the serrated back of a gigantic alligator broke the surface.

Flavius hesitated. He would almost rather face the war party than plunge back into the heart of darkness. Almost, but not quite. An arrow that nearly clipped an ear added incentive. He descended, careful not to slip, especially at the bottom where water lapped at the grass. They had to bear to the left, to a spur of dry land that pointed into the swamp like a huge accusing finger. It, in turn, linked the hill to the trail they had been on since they began.

Davy twisted. Warriors were above, silhouetted against the sky. Five only. The rest must be tending to the wounded man, he reckoned.

"Do we make a stand?" Flavius inquired, praying they would not.

The idea had merit. The only way the Indians could get at them was by crossing the spur. Or so it appeared. But Davy would not put it past the warriors to know of another way. The swamp was their home. They had explored every nook, every sheltered cove.

Another factor was advice given to him by his father, John, who had been a Ranger during the revolution against the British. "Never let yourself be hemmed in by an enemy. Always fight in the open, where you can retreat if you have to. Learn from history. Remember Leonidas at Thermopylae."

Davy had taken the advice to heart. "No, we keep going," he now answered. The trees grew so close in, boughs overstretched the path, forming a green tunnel. They sped on in premature twilight, Davy sorely wishing it were the real thing. He reloaded Liz as he ran, stopping briefly once to feed black powder into the muzzle.

Flavius grew more encouraged with every minute the warriors did not show. He tried to convince himself the Indians were afraid of guns and would let them alone. To believe the worst was over.

"Did you hear that?" Davy asked. A trilling cry that resembled a bird's, but was not, had warbled to the south, to be mimicked by a similar cry to the north.

"They're signaling."

"The rush will come soon," Davy predicted. It made sense for the war party to strike well before the sun set so they

31

could bear their victims—or bloody scalps and body parts—to their village in triumph. He changed his mind about making a stand. Casting about, he spotted a small island in the center of a broad pool. "There," he declared, stopping and pointing.

"There what?"

"We fight." Davy held Liz aloft and entered the water.

Flavius balked. Making a stand had been his idea, but he would rather step barefoot over red-hot coals than wade into a pool that might be teeming with gators and serpents. "Maybe there's a better spot."

"No time to search. Hurry."

"But—" Flavius said, falling silent when Davy dismissed his objection with a wave. Crockett had made up his mind, and once a member of the Crockett clan had settled on a course of action, that was all there was to it. Often Flavius had wondered if all Irish were so unbearably stubborn, or whether the Crocketts enjoyed a monopoly.

The water was cool and refreshing, but Flavius barely noticed. He was wary of ripples that marked the passage of something under the surface. Something that swam toward them. Hiking his rifle so he could bash whatever it was the moment it appeared, he chortled when a frog rose up out of the soup and then quickly dived again.

Davy did not like it when the water rose past his knees. Should either of his pistols become wet, long, precious minutes would be needed to dry them. As the level climbed, he slowed. It would not do to step into a deep hole. He picked his way with caution, probing with his toes.

More birdcalls twittered on the hot wind. Flavius saw stealthy movement along the trail and snapped up his rifle, but the warrior was gone in a twinkling. Straying wide of his friend, Flavius backed toward the island. Suddenly a heel stepped into empty space. He tried to right himself, but his own weight pulled him downward. His foot connected with slippery muck. Bracing his leg, he attempted to lever upward, but it was like trying to tread on liquid ice. The mud gave way. His whole body tilted.

Davy heard a splash and shifted. The water was almost to his friend's waist. Another couple of heartbeats and Flavius would go all the way under. Lunging, Davy grasped him by the shoulder, digging his fingers into the buckskin.

"Damn!" Flavius squawked, pumping his left leg to no avail. He could not gain solid purchase, and he was slowly but inevitably pulling Davy toward the hole too. "Let go!"

"No!" Davy dug in his heels, refusing to admit defeat. They could not afford to render any of their guns useless. "Try harder!"

Flavius steeled his right leg, wrenched his hips forward, and succeeded in rising a few inches. Enough for his other foot to brush against something solid, something that offered salvation. He stepped directly on it and rose even higher. "I'm safe now!" he exclaimed, only to have the object he had trod on abruptly explode into motion and wriggle out from under him. A gator!

Davy threw himself at the island, hauling Flavius along. Several yards away a reptilian snout reared up out of the deep, but did not approach. Keeping one eye on the pool's lord and master, Davy forged the remaining ten feet and gained solid ground.

"We made it!" Flavis said. Freed, he moved away from the water's edge in case the alligator came after them. He checked his pistols to verify they were dry. His powder horn was also untouched, but the bottom of his ammo pouch was slightly damp. It contained his lead balls, which could be quickly wiped dry.

Davy made a circuit of the island. Twenty-two steps. Four slender trees and a hump of earth were the only shelter from the rain of arrows sure to deluge them once the war party was in position. Already he glimpsed warriors fanning out, surrounding the pool. Taking a position on his knees behind the hummock, he stared at a shaft of sunlight that spilled onto the water and lent it a golden glow.

Flavius was too nervous to keep still. He paced from tree to tree, the alligator forgotten as he saw more and more warriors arrive.

"Never thought it would end like this," Davy remarked.

"Me either," Flavius said. "I always figured to die in bed of old age. Or maybe to be nagged to death by my wife. Not to end up with more quills than a porcupine." The last was meant as a joke, but neither of them cracked a grin.

Davy faced him. "I want you to know something. Of all the friends I've ever had, you're the best. You have more sand than an hourglass. If I had my life to live over again, I would still be honored to have you at my side."

A lump formed in Flavius's throat. The Irishman had never bared his emotions so plainly before. It showed how serious their plight was. Their luck had finally played out; they were at the end of their string. Coughing, he answered, "I feel the same, hoss. I just hope the Almighty sees fit to pair us up in the next life as well."

Whatever response Davy was on the verge of making was cut off by fierce whoops on all sides. The Indians were attacking!

Chapter Three

At the signal, the war party burst into the open. Surging toward the pool, many let fly long shafts that buzzed like angry hornets. Davy Crockett barely had time to holler, ''Take cover!'' before the small island was peppered. Some arrows struck the trees, others imbedded themselves in the earth. One smacked into the soil close to Davy's shoulder.

Flavius ducked down behind a bole. He brought up his rifle, but a shaft rammed the barrel, deflecting the gun before he could shoot.

The deluge of arrows was intended to keep the Tennesseans pinned down while other warriors barreled into the water and converged.

Davy raised his head, and saw a brawny warrior with a war club lumbering toward him. He extended Liz to take aim. Out of the corner of an eye he noticed another warrior on the north bank, one with the long piece of cane. The man raised an end to his mouth and pointed the other end at *him*.

Davy could not say what made him drop flat. He had never

seen Indians use such a weapon. Maybe it was a dim memory of his childhood when he and friends had whittled smaller versions from hollow reeds. Whatever the case, he dropped in the nick of time, for no sooner had he done so than a six-inch dart smacked into the earth above him. He yanked it out, saw a long wicked, tip discolored at the end—perhaps by a poison the Indians had applied—and threw it aside.

The man was inserting another dart into the blowgun. Of all the warriors, Davy rated this one the most dangerous. The blowgun was silent, yet incredibly effective, and no doubt highly lethal. The dart flew so fast, it was next to invisible. Davy did not want to worry about being hit while he was busy fighting, so without delay he raised his rifle and fired. The ball cored the man's cranium from front to back, the deadly blowgun falling into weeds.

Davy was not given a moment's respite. Arrows still rained down all around. And six or seven warriors were halfway to the island. He heard Flavius's rifle crack, saw a painted enemy pitch into the pool. Setting Liz down, Davy drew both pistols.

The brawny warrior with the war club was in the lead. Wagging his weapon, he yipped like a demented coyote and motioned for his fellows to hurry.

Was he their leader? Davy wondered. A chief maybe? Davy brought a flintlock to bear. As he had learned during the Creek War, slaying a chief often caused the rest to withdraw.

Suddenly the pool bubbled and frothed. In the excitement, Davy had forgotten about the alligator. The scaly brute had submerged when the Indians entered its lair, but now it heaved up out of the murk, its massive jaws clamping onto a hapless victim. The man screeched, then thrust a glittering knife at the alligator's head, again and again and again. Other warriors rushed to help as the alligator tried to pull its prey under.

For the moment, the attackers were not interested in Davy and Flavius. Clubs and knives flashing, they vented their fury on the reptile. It went into a roll, or tried to, its jagged tail whipping like a snake gone amok. Two warriors were bowled over. But the rest never hesitated. They tore into the creature with a vengeance. One sank a blade into an eye. Another slashed the gator's throat.

Meanwhile, Flavius was reloading his rifle just as fast as his fingers could fly. He was scared, but he did not show it. If his time had come, he would die as he had always been told a man should. Bravely. Without whining or moaning or whimpering. He saw Davy reloading, and blustered, ''We'll give them what for, eh, partner?''

Davy smiled encouragement. The battle in the pool was winding down. The alligator was motionless. Its jaws had been pried wide and the stricken man was being ushered back to shore.

The downpour of shafts and darts had temporarily stopped while the gator was dealt with. Now it resumed. A dart clipped the whangs on Davy's hunting shirt. Bringing up Liz, he shot the warrior responsible.

The man with the war club was out in front again. He had a nasty scar on his left cheek that zigzagged from just under his eye to below his chin. Dark eyes aglitter with raw spite, he glared at Davy as if daring Davy to fire at him. So Davy did. At the pistol's retort, the brawny warrior jerked backward and twisted.

Davy started to shift toward another foe. He figured the brawny man was as good as dead. No one could survive a direct hit to the chest. A bellow of outrage proved him wrong. Stupefied, he watched the warrior straighten, heft the heavy war club, and charge again.

Davy did not know what to think. His flintlock had not misfired or fouled. The lead ball had flown straight and true.

The warrior should be floating in the pool. Yet the man did not seem the least bit fazed.

Flavius Harris had witnessed the event, and was dumfounded. It reminded him of a tale he'd heard during the campaign against the Creeks, about a noted warrior called Red Shirt who hated all whites. As the story went, Red Shirt had claimed to be invincible. Thanks to a talisman or charm given to him by a medicine man, Red Shirt was supposed to be bullet-proof.

It was ridiculous, of course. No one was immune to bullets. Yet the men around the campfire that night had been in a battle against Red Shirt's band. And they swore by all that was holy that several shots had been fired at the Creek chief and not one had had an effect. None of the balls had so much as broken the skin.

Flavius had scoffed. There must be a logical explanation, he had replied. When he suggested they'd missed, unflattering comments had been made about his mother, and he'd been told in no uncertain terms that they had been too close to miss. Anyway, some of them had seen Red Shirt pushed back by the force of the bullets and then keep on coming. How could Flavius explain that?

He couldn't. He never had understood how Indian hoodoo was supposed to work. Indians who carried special charms to ward off injury or death were fooling themselves. The only things that really worked were crucifixes. Or, sometimes, graven images of religious figures.

Now, Flavius gaped at the onrushing warrior who had shrugged off Davy's shot, and gulped. He aimed Matilda.

Abruptly, a new element was added to the conflict. There were four distinct blasts, one after the other, from the vegetation to the northeast. With each shot a warrior fell, either on the shore or in the water. Those remaining swiveled to confront this new threat, but at a roar from their leader they hastened to the west.

Davy could have dropped one or two, but he didn't. He had never shot an enemy in the back, and he was not about to start. Whoever was concealed in the undergrowth did not share his outlook, however. Guns boomed several more times, and at each sound an Indian fell.

Flavius wanted to whoop for joy. They were saved! The only question was: Who had done the saving? He did not show himself for fear it might be other Indians who wanted scalps of their own.

The last of the war party disappeared. Snapping brush marked their passage. As the sounds faded, the undergrowth to the east parted and out walked two men.

Davy slowly rose. Surprise was piling on surprise. One of the newcomers was a tall white man in buckskins, the other a black in homespun clothes. Each held a pair of smoking rifles. They came to the pool, the white man stepping over a warrior who was still alive. Hearing the man groan, the newcomer handed his rifles to the black fellow, then drew the biggest knife Davy had ever set eyes on. The blade alone was nearly a foot long. It sported a plain wooden handle.

Stooping, the white man gripped the warrior by the hair, wrenched to one side to better expose the neck, and slit the warrior's throat with a single short swipe. Just like that. Wiping the polished blade clean on the warrior's loincloth, the tall man uncoiled and walked to the water's edge. "Good thing we heard the ruckus or you'd be buzzard bait along about now."

Davy, gazing at the ruptured throat, simply nodded.

The tall man smiled. He was a strapping specimen. Broad shoulders tapered to a slim waist. Deep-set eyes were an unusual shade of blue, almost blue-gray. Chestnut-brown hair framed a handsome face dominated by a high, wide forehead and a strong chin. Bushy sideburns angled halfway down his jaw. Putting his hands on his hips, he addressed Davy. "Is that a dead coon you have on your head, friend?"

"We call it a coonskin cap where I come from," Crockett answered.

"Ah. And where might that be? From your accent, I take it maybe Kentucky or Tennessee."

Davy confirmed it was the latter. Moving toward the pool, he introduced himself, then Flavius. "We're on our way to New Orleans," he mentioned. "Those Indians you chased off stole our horses."

The man's features hardened. "The Karankawas," he said bitterly. "They've caused me no end of grief the past few years." He glowered in the direction they had taken. "That was Snake Strangler and his bunch."

"Snake Strangler?" Davy repeated. An unusual name.

"A cottonmouth crawled into his father's lodge when he was four. Somehow or other, the boy got a grip on its neck and choked the snake to death."

"Did the snake give him that scar?"

The tall man patted the big knife at his hip. "No, that was me. We don't exactly see eye-to-eye on a few things. He thinks his people own this swamp, and I say a man has the right to go where he damn well pleases. One of these days we'll settle our differences, one way or another."

Davy waded across, Flavius right behind. The alligator floated belly-up. Beside it bobbed a Karankawa with a new nostril. "I reckon we're in your debt," he mentioned as he emerged. The black man was busy reloading the four rifles.

"Think nothing of it, friend," the tall man said, offering his hand. "You'd have done the same for me, if I'm any judge." He shook. "I'm James, by the way."

Davy made two observations. First, their savior was immensely strong. Second, the man had made it a point not to reveal his last name. Why? Was he a fugitive from justice? A brigand? Perhaps one of the freebooters who had plagued Texas in recent years, looting and killing to their heart's content?

James indicated the black man. "This is Sam. He's been looking after me since I was knee-high to a nanny goat."

Davy thought it strange that anyone as powerful and imposing as James needed someone for a wet nurse. Especially since Sam did not appear to be much older than James himself. "Pleased to meet you."

The black rose. "Here you go, Master Jim. Loaded, she is." He handed over a rifle. "What's next? Do we get the rest on the move before that awful Snake Strangler comes back with his whole tribe?"

Davy looked at James. "Master?"

"My father bought Sam for me when I was a sprout. We've pretty much grown up together. I think of him more as a friend than a slave, but the stubborn cuss won't stop calling me that even though I've threatened to cut out his tongue if he doesn't."

Sam showed his teeth. "Pay me no mind, Mr. Crockett. It's my way of remindin' Jimmy he can't walk on water, no matter how high an opinion he has of himself."

"Oh. I think I understand."

Flavius sure didn't. At a loss for words, he had not said a thing since the newcomers showed up. He gazed to the west, fretting that the war party might double back and catch them off guard.

James was studying the Irishman. "You say that you're on your way to New Orleans? Sort of off the beaten path, aren't you? No one in their right mind tries to cross the swamp when there's a perfectly good road from Nacogdoches east."

"I was hoping to shave some time off the journey," Davy disclosed, and patted Flavius on the shoulder. "My friend and I have been away from home much too long. We have a hankering to get back before our womenfolk forget what we look like."

"Well, without horses you won't shave any time," James said. "And alone, you might not make it at all. The Karan-

41

kawas will be up in arms. Snake Strangler won't rest until he's made gator food of all of us."

Davy scratched his chin. "Are you proposing we join forces?"

"There's strength in numbers," James said. "I have two other men working for me, both good with a gun and a knife. You're welcome to tag along so long as you remember I'm in charge and hold up your end of the chores."

Gazing beyond the pair, Davy asked, "Where are these other gents?"

"About a mile from here," James said. "Sam and I were hunting for a member of our party who wandered off and got lost when we heard the hullabaloo."

Flavius's interest perked up. "This fellow you're hunting wouldn't happen to be a black feller? Wearing a danged peculiar animal hide? A hide with spots?"

James and Sam swapped looks. "That would be the one," the former said. "You've seen him? Where at? The sooner we fetch him back, the sooner we can be on our way. And the safer we'll be."

Davy did not like being the bearer of bad tidings. "Your friend is dead. Snakebit. We were going to bury him, but the Indians had other ideas. They carved out his heart—"

An oath escaped James and he flushed beet-red with anger. "Damn Snake Strangler all to Hell! The Karankawas consider the heart a delicacy. By eating it, they think they take on the qualities of the heart's owner."

A queasy sensation took root in the pit of Flavius's stomach. "So those tall tales we heard are true? The Karankawas are cannibals?"

James cradled the rifle and accepted another from Sam. "Not in the strict sense of the word, no. They won't eat every part of you. Just the juiciest tidbits." Gruff laughter rumbled from his keg of a chest.

"That makes me feel a whole lot better," Flavius said.

When, in truth, he felt immensely worse. The notion of being devoured by wild beasts was horrendous enough; the idea of being eaten by *people* was downright sickening.

Davy fell into step behind James. "You haven't mentioned what you're doing here. Our excuse is that we were in a hurry. What's yours?" When there was no response, he said, "It sounds as if you know all about the Karankawas. Yet you're willing to try and cross cannibal country? Is it me, or do you have a secret death wish?"

The tall man snickered. "Not at all. I had no choice." Staring out over the unending swampland, he said somberly, "A man does what he has to do. In my case, it made good business sense."

"What kind of business are you in?" Davy casually inquired.

"You'll find out soon enough," was the puzzling response.

Flavius observed one of the fallen warriors move weakly. "I think some of the Injuns are still alive. Shouldn't we do something? Put them out of their misery maybe?"

"Let them suffer," James declared.

"Isn't that a mite harsh?" Davy asked.

"Is it?" the tall frontiersman countered. "I say let them rot. Buzzards have to eat too, don't they?" He forestalled further debate by picking up the pace.

Davy was trying to place their benefactor by his accent. Louisiana would be his first guess, Mississippi or maybe Arkansas his second.

James moved with the fluid grace of a panther, as much at home in the swamp as one of the great cats would be. Despite the growing darkness, he confidently led them along a winding maze of game trails until at length they came to a large clearing, and a camp.

A telltale acrid scent of wood smoke had given Davy forewarning. The two men James had mentioned were crouched near a fire, sipping coffee. But they were not the only ones

43

present. Sprawled in exhaustion on both sides of the glade were twenty men and women. Blacks, linked ten in a row by lengths of chain shackled to their ankles.

"Slaves!" Flavius blurted.

Most of the men wore loincloths similar to the man the Tennesseans had encountered earlier. The women wore short leather skirts, but were stark naked above the waist. Copper rings adorned their noses and ears. Mud layered their legs, and their bodies bore scuffs and scratches. Davy scanned their haggard faces, reading the misery in their eyes, and frowned. "So this explains it. You're a slave runner."

"I get the impression you don't approve," James said.

Davy had never much liked the concept of one human being owning another. Back in 1808 a federal law had been passed banning the importation of slaves, but the trade flourished nonetheless. Slave smuggling was practiced all along the Gulf of Mexico and up the Atlantic coast as far north as Virginia, or so he'd heard tell.

The two men by the small fire rose. Scruffy characters whose caps and seedy clothes identified them as river rats, they glared at Davy and Flavius in open hostility. "What the hell is this?" rasped the one on the left. "Where did you find these bumpkins?"

Flavius bristled and took a step. "I'd be careful who I insulted, mister. After what we've been through, we're not in the mood to be trifled with."

The other river rat tittered. "Better watch out, Arlo. This fat fool thinks he's tough. Maybe we should teach him a lesson, eh?" A flick of the wrist, and a stiletto appeared in the man's right hand. "Want me to cut him into little pieces and feed him to the snappers?"

Davy was set to intervene, but James beat him to it. Striding forward, the tall man rested a palm on that big knife and said ominously, "If there's any cutting to be done, I'll do it.

Put that toothpick of yours away, Sedge. Or would you rather match blades with me?''

Sedge smirked slyly, then winked at Arlo. ''Sure, Jimbo, sure. Whatever you want. I'm not crazy enough to challenge you. I've seen what you can do with that short sword.''

Arlo rose on his toes to peer into the benighted woods. ''Say? Where's the darkie who got away? I thought you were going to bring him back?''

''He's dead,'' James reported.

''Damn,'' Arlo swore. ''That's one hundred and forty dollars gone, just like that.'' He snapped his fingers. ''I hope that doesn't mean our cut will be less. It's not our fault he slipped his shackle. If that boy of yours had done his job—''

James loomed over the river rat, his countenance crackling with wrath. ''It's *my* money, not yours. And don't blame Sam. He checked the shackles before they bedded down, just like he always does.''

Arlo mustered a bleak smile. ''Don't get your dander up. I'm not layin' fault on anyone. None of us noticed that darkie's ankle was so thin, or we'd have tied him too.''

Sedge laughed. ''So we lost one. So what? We have twenty left. At the going rate, they'll bring in close to twelve thousand dollars. Not bad for three weeks' work, eh?'' Nudging Arlo, he sipped from his battered tin cup.

It was rare for Davy to take an instant dislike to someone, but he intensely distrusted both river rats. Their ilk were all too common in waterfront dives along the Mississippi, backstabbers who would kill a man for pocket change if they thought they could do it without being caught. Why James had seen fit to ally himself with such vermin was a mystery.

Arlo had money uppermost on his mind. ''What about the bumpkins?'' he asked. ''I hope you don't plan to cut them in? Sedge and me ain't takin' any less than what we agreed.''

James moved to the coffeepot. ''Did I say you would get

any less? I'm a man of my word, Kastner. Five percent is the amount we agreed on. Five percent is what each of you will receive.''

Davy did some mental calculations. Six hundred dollars apiece was what it came to. Double a year's earnings for most folks. Extravagant pay, but given the perils, the pair must earn every cent.

Flavius looked at the wretches in irons. *Twelve thousand dollars* they were worth! A king's ransom. More money than he had made in his whole life. No wonder smugglers were willing to take enormous risks to deal in black ivory, as the trade was known. A man could amass a fortune in no time.

Flavius had never had much of a hunger to be rich himself. He'd always been content with his lot in life, making the best of what it had to offer. Which annoyed Matilda no end. After they had been wed about three years, she'd shocked him one day by saying she had always wanted to be wealthy. ''Then why in tarnation did you marry me?'' he had responded. He should have known he was in trouble when she'd sweetly asked, ''You don't want to be rich?'' Without thinking, he'd replied, ''You must be joshing. What chance do I have? I'm not about to work myself to a frazzle for something that will never happen. So why bother?'' For his stupidity he had been treated to the tongue-lashing to end all tongue-lashings, a verbal blistering that began with, ''A jackass has more brains than you!'' and ended with the woman's argument of last resort, ''Why I married you, I will *never* know!''

Davy reached for a cup that lay on a flat rock, but Sam snatched it it up, filled it, and held it out for him to take.

''Here you go, sir.''

''Thanks. But don't call me sir. We're all equals here.''

The river rats cackled with glee. Sedge slapped his thigh, spilling some of his coffee, then declared, ''Did you hear this lout, Arlo? He thinks whites and darkies are the same.''

Arlo snorted. ''Some yacks ain't got the brains God gave

a turnip." He wagged a finger at Davy. "I don't know what you use for eyes, mister. But if you'll take a gander at those Negroes yonder, you'll see they're a lot different from us ordinary folks."

Davy looked, all right. He saw human beings who had been pushed to the limits of their endurance. Innocents who had been ripped from their homeland and dragged to waiting ships. Shattered spirits who had endured a torturous sea voyage and wound up on a foreign shore. Broken men and women who would spend the rest of their lives in servitude. They, and their children, and their children's children. He looked, and was sick to his soul.

"Why, I do believe this fella is about to cry," Sedge said.

"It's as my ma used to say," Arlo remarked. "There's a simpleton born every minute."

Maybe it was the ordeal with the Karankawas. Maybe it was the loss of the horses. Maybe being hungry and tired was to blame. Or perhaps it was a combination of all those factors that triggered an explosion deep within the Irishman. For before he quite realized what he was doing, he had shot to his feet, taken a step, and hurled the coffee in his cup into Arlo's face.

Shrieking like a painter, the river rat leaped up. He sputtered, wiped a sleeve across his eyes and cheeks, and bellowed, "Son of a bitch! You damn near blinded me! I'll gut you for that!"

Sedge leaned over to grab a rifle propped on a log. The metallic click of a trigger being cocked transformed him to marble.

"Simmer down, all of you," James ordered. "There will be no shooting. Not unless you *want* Snake Strangler to pinpoint where we are." Sidling around the fire to where he could see all of them clearly, he added, "It's a long way to New Orleans. We'd better learn to get along or none of us will get out of the swamp alive."

47

Coffee dripped from Arlo's chin and dribbled down his neck. He glanced at the tall frontiersman's rifle, then at the Irishman. "I never say no to a man holdin' a gun on me. But this ain't over, stranger. Mark my words. You'll regret being born before this is done."

Davy had no doubt the river rat would carry through on the threat. But he didn't care. There was only so much abuse a man could abide if he really was a man. Refilling his cup, he sat back down.

Flavius Harris was fit to cry. *Why couldn't things go right for once?* Just when he thought they had been saved and the worst was over, fickle Fate had thrown them in with a slaver and a pair of rabid cutthroats.

Flavius was beginning to think somebody up above didn't like him.

Chapter Four

By noon the next day they had covered a mere seven miles.

At first light they were up. The river rats rekindled the fire, and Sam made coffee. Davy Crockett was mildly surprised and pleased when James made it a point to hand out a piece of jerked venison to each of the slaves. It wasn't much, but at least the blacks were being fed.

Three large leather pouches were packed with the jerky and other essential items, one pouch carried by each of the slavers. They were also armed to the teeth. Walking armories, with two rifles apiece, one of which was normally slung over a shoulder, as well as three pistols and two knives. Except James, who only sported the one knife, the big one with the wide, thick blade.

Davy was curious about it, and when they stopped for brief rest at mid-morning he idly commented, "That's some pig-sticker you've got there. I don't believe I've seen it's like anywhere."

James slid the weapon out with a flourish. "You haven't.

It's one of a kind. Made for me by my brother, Rezin,'' he proudly revealed. ''He's always tinkering with knives, trying to improve them.''

''Is he a blacksmith?'' Davy asked. A logical question, since only a smith could custom forge such a weapon.

James chuckled. ''No, no. Rezin is a lot like me. A bit of a rogue. Part scoundrel, some might say. He sketched how he wanted the knife to be, then had the smith on our plantation make it.'' James ran a finger along a thin guard that separated the handle from the blade. ''This is his main improvement. To protect the hand.''

Davy had to admit it was a clever notion. No one had ever thought to add a guard to a hunting knife before.

''A wild bull deserves some of the credit,'' James had gone on. ''We used to hunt them when we were younger.'' Pausing, he gazed into the distance, as if seeing his past mirrored in the clouds. ''You know how boys are. We were ornery as could be back then. Gators, gar, you name it, we hunted it. Our favorites were the huge steers that run wild in these swamps. Our friends would just shoot them, but where's the thrill in that?''

''How did you do it then?'' Davy inquired.

''We'd get in close, use a rope, and trip them. Once they were down, we'd run in with our knives and stab them before they could gore us with their horns. That was about as fair as we could make it.''

Davy had never heard of such a thing. Dangerous game was not to be taken lightly. It gave him new insight into the man's personality.

''Anyway, one time Rezin lassoed a big, wicked bull. He got the brute down, then sprang in to finish it off. But when he stabbed it in the neck, his butcher knife struck bone. His hand slipped off the hilt and he nearly severed two of his fingers. Hellacious cut. That gave him the inspiration to add a guard.''

"Do tell," Davy said. "It sounds as if your boyhood was uncommonly wild and woolly."

"Oh, no more so than most other boys who live in the wilderness," James responded, and waxed nostalgic. "It was a fine life. My parents loved us dearly. My mother was religious and read to us regularly from Scripture, but at that age we were more interested in tomfoolery than the Ten Commandments."

Davy recollected his own childhood, and the many hours he had spent in the woods rather than going to school or doing his chores. He grinned. "We were a lot alike, you and I."

"I could tell the moment we met," James said. "You should have been with us on the plantation. We had a grand old time. My favorite sport was to ride alligators."

"Wait a second," Davy said. "I didn't come down with yesterday's rain, you know."

"Honest to God. We would jump on their backs and ride them until they were tuckered out. The trick is to hold onto their upper jaws so they can't go under the water, while at the same time you gouge your thumbs into their eyes so they can't see."

Davy had to concede the trick might work, but for the life of him he couldn't imagine anyone being reckless enough to try. "You could have been killed."

James shrugged his broad shoulders. "We never know from one day to the next if we'll be alive to greet the next dawn. So why not make the most of life before our time is up?" He rose and adjusted his leather pouch. "I've always lived life to the fullest, friend. And to do that, a person needs money. Lots and lots of money."

"So is that why you deal in black ivory?"

"Exactly. Rezin, me, and one other brother went into the business together a couple of years ago. After this trip, I figure we'll have over sixty thousand dollars to our name."

Davy whistled softly.

51

"I'm partial to the good life," James elaborated. "Fine clothes, fine carriages, fine women, and fine food. When we finally have enough to suit me, I plan to move to New Orleans and set myself up in elegant style."

"How much is enough?"

"Oh, I don't rightly know. Maybe a hundred thousand."

Davy nodded at the blacks, who sat in the shade of a cypress. "And those poor people?"

The tall man's brow furrowed. "What about them? I treat them decently. You've seen for yourself that I don't whip them or starve them or abuse the women."

"And once we've made it through the swamp?"

"What else? They'll be sold to the highest bidders at a secret auction. They'll join hundreds of others just like them on plantations all across the South. How their new masters treat them is out of my control." Pumping an arm, James called out, "Let's move out, men. Daylight's a wasting."

They had been on the go for ten minutes or so when Davy realized something. The tall man had said it would be a "secret" auction. But why a secret one, when slaves were sold openly all the time? The government had banned the importing of new slaves, not the exchange of slaves already here. Newly smuggled slaves were routinely given forged papers that established they had been in the country for years.

For this bunch to be sold at a secret auction implied there was more to the situation than a mere smuggling operation. But Davy could not guess what it might be. He kept his ears pricked for tidbits of information, but the slavers did not chat much on the trail. And Arlo and Sedge would not talk to him anyway. They glared at him all morning, nursing grudges from the night before.

Which was too bad. Davy hoped to learn James's last name, learn more about their operation. Not that he would turn them in. What they did was their business, even if he didn't approve.

It was how things were done on the frontier. One of the earliest lessons Davy's pa had taught him was that a man always minded his own affairs. Never, ever, should he meddle in anyone else's.

Still, Davy could not help but feel sorry for the blacks. And to wish there was something he could do on their behalf.

It was strange how life worked sometimes. All the slaves he had seen over the years, and he never given much thought to their welfare. Never thought twice about the conditions under which they toiled. Experience, he wryly reflected, sure enough had a way of sweating the fat from a man's brain.

Glancing back, Davy smiled at Flavius, who returned the favor.

But Flavius did not really feel like smiling. He was hot and sore and hungry and thirsty. And he was growing to hate the swamp. Insects always swarmed about his face. Mosquitoes constantly stung him. Serpents were forever slithering out from underfoot. And there was the constant threat of gators.

It didn't help that they fought shy of the main trail. Instead of being dry and safe, they threaded through the heart of the swamp along a route apparently known only to the slavers. At times the ground was solid, but all too often they were up to their knees in rank swamp water or muck.

Flavius was in dire dread of being snakebit or pulled under by an alligator. Once, when he stepped over a log and something skittered out from under it and shot past his foot, he jumped and yelped like a kicked puppy. But it turned out to be a measly salamander. The river rats guffawed at his expense. Over the next several hours they mocked him, one or the other hopping into the air, squeaking like a mouse, and flailing his arms as if in mortal terror. Flavius was not amused.

Nor was Davy. But for the sake of keeping the peace he held his tongue. When James called another halt along about two in the afternoon, Davy made it a point to sit near him. "Mind if I ask you a question?"

"Ask whatever you want. Just don't expect an answer if it's too personal."

Davy poked a thumb at where Arlo and Sedge sat. "Why on earth did you hook up with a pair like that? They're as low-down as a worm in a wagon track and as slick as an onion. You might as well team up with a pair of rabid dogs."

"You think I don't know that?" James said, and exhaled. "Believe you me, if I had my druthers, I'd be shed of them so fast your head would swim. But there's that old saw about beggars can't be choosers. I had no choice."

"It won't wash."

"Think so, do you?" James regarded the duo with distaste. "I'll have you know I scoured every tavern and saloon along the waterfront for men brave enough to go with me this trip. Only a few had the gumption. And believe it or not, Sedge and his cousin were the pick of the litter."

"Some litter," Davy scoffed. "Why didn't your brothers come?"

"Rezin had important business to attend to. John's wife was ailing. So it was just Sam and me. But the way Snake Strangler has been acting up, I decided to bring extra men along. Just in case."

"My grandma used to say that when you frolic with the Devil, you're going to have demons for company."

James grinned. "Nicely put." He lowered his voice even more. "Just between you and me, Tennessee, I'm glad you and your friend joined us. Having to watch my back every hour of the day and night gets mighty tiresome."

"Tell you what. You help watch my back and I'll help watch yours. The same with Flavius and Sam."

"Agreed."

Davy leaned against a tree, pondering. Here he was, siding with a slaver, when his conscience told him to have nothing to do with the man. But he had taken a shine to James. The mysterious frontiersman was right; they had a lot in common. Backwoodsmen born and bred, they shared a special bond.

And too, James had a personality hard to dislike. Forceful yet friendly, commanding yet generous. The sort of man it would do to ride the river with, as the Texicans liked to say. If not for the business of the slaves, Davy would like him even more.

Everyone had flaws, though. Everyone. Davy's was his wanderlust, his compulsive curiosity to see what lay over the next horizon. Flavius was too timid for his own good, but otherwise as fine a fellow as ever trod the earth. James, it was quite plain, craved money above all else, and was willing to work the shady side of the law to acquire a lot of it.

Suddenly, crackling broke out in the undergrowth. Davy pushed to his feet, his hands falling to his flintlocks.

"It's only Sam," James said.

Out came the black man, in a state of excited agitation. "They're after us, Master Jimmy, just as you said they would be. I climbed that tree like you wanted and saw them about a mile back."

"How many?"

"Ten or more would be my guess. It's awful hard to say, them being so far away and all."

Arlo and Sedge hurried over. So did Flavius. James swore, then said, "The Karankawas are hot on our trail. They'll catch us unless we make it too costly for them. So the rest of you will push on while I do just that."

"Alone?" Davy said, and found himself adding, "The odds are too great. I'll stick by your side to even them some."

Dismay seared Flavius. Gripping his partner's wrist, he steered the Irishman to one side, out of earshot, and demanded, "What's gotten into you? Why risk your hide for a man you hardly know?"

"Our lives are at stake too," Davy reminded him. "The

Karankawas nearly made worm food of us once. We'll have the whole tribe down on our heads if we don't stop them while we still can." He leaned closer. "Don't fret. I'll be fine. I want you to go with the others."

"Not on your life. Where you go, I go."

"Listen. Someone has to keep an eye on those two ruffians. They're not to be trusted any further than either of us could chuck a black bear." Davy squeezed his friend's shoulder. "It's in both our interests to help James out. He can get us safely to New Orleans. And remember, he saved our lives yesterday. We owe him."

Against Flavius's better judgment, he agreed to do as Crockett requested. "But you had better not get yourself killed or I'll never forgive you."

With some misgivings Davy stood in the center of the clearing and watched the column file off. Flavius and Sam brought up the rear, Flavius waving until a bend hid them. Hoping he had not made a grave mistake, Davy hefted Liz. "Ready when you are."

James was honing his big knife. "We have time yet." Looking up directly into Davy's eyes, he asked, "Can I trust you, Tennessee? Really and truly trust you?"

"Yes," Davy said, and meant it.

"I guess you've noticed that I haven't told you my last name. Wondered why?"

"You must have your reasons."

"I do. I didn't want you to know who I was so you couldn't report me to the federal authorities if you learned the truth." James stopping stroking the long blade over the whetstone. "Those slaves aren't ordinary slaves. They're stolen."

"Who did you steal them from?"

"I didn't. Lafitte did."

"Lafitte? Not Jean Lafitte the pirate?" Davy was astonished. Everyone knew of the notorious privateer who had helped Andrew Jackson defeat the British at the Battle of New Orleans.

James nodded. "Jean is a close friend of mine. I've often been a guest of his at Campeachy."

Davy was trying to recall all the facts he could about Lafitte. Years ago the man had taken over the smuggling operation out of Grande Terre Isle in the Bay of Barataria. At one time, it was rumored, he'd had over a thousand men under him, and over fifty fine ships that roamed the high seas seeking plunder.

Shortly before the Battle of New Orleans, fearing Lafitte might go over to the British, the American Navy had attacked the pirate's stronghold. Lafitte had never lifted a finger to defend himself. Nor had he allowed his men to fire on an American flag. So the pirates had fled and their sanctuary had been destroyed.

Lafitte had gone to meet General Andrew Jackson personally, and offered his services in return for a pardon for him and his followers. After the war, the pirate had set up another base on an island off the Texas coast. Campeachy, he had called it.

"We have a lucrative arrangement," James went on. "Lafitte's men board Spanish and British slavers, take the slaves, and bring them to Jean's stronghold. My brothers and I then smuggle them from Campeachy into Louisiana. We pay Jean an average of one hundred and forty dollars for a healthy black man." He slid the knife into its sheath. "They fetch upwards of eight hundred at auction. So Jean makes money, we make money, and no one is hurt."

"It doesn't bother you? Selling people as if they were cattle?"

"No," James said. Frowning, he sighed, and his shoulders slumped. "All right. Maybe a little. But I need a lot of money, and I want it fast. This is the best way to obtain it."

"The ends justify the means? Is that how it is?"

The tall man grew indignant. "Damn it, Tennessee! Who are you to sit in judgment? The slave trade has been around for hundreds of years. Hell, George Washington and Thomas Jefferson owned slaves, and they were Presidents. I'm not doing anything the leaders of our own country haven't done."

"They *owned* slaves, true, but they didn't *smuggle* any."

"A shady distinction, if you ask me."

Davy changed the subject. "Why are you telling me all this?"

It was a full half a minute before the other man answered. "Odd, isn't it? We've only just met, yet I feel as if I could trust you with my life. What I've told you just now could get me hung if you reported it, but something tells me you won't." He paused. "So I might as well go whole hog. My last name is Bowie."

"James Bowie," Davy said, grinning. "Pleased to make your acquaintance. Again."

They clasped hands warmly. Davy was about to assure his newfound friend that he would indeed never betray Bowie's confidence when a bird twittered to the west. A cry Davy had heard before—when the Karankawas were hot on his trail.

Bowie whirled and darted in among the trees. "Hurry."

Davy followed suit, the tail on his coonskin cap flopping against an ear. Veering to the left, they jogged twenty yards, to a log that lay near the clearing's perimeter. James dropped onto his knees, rested his rifle on top, and whispered, "Snake Strangler is the one we want. Kill him, and the rest will take it as a bad omen and leave us be."

Davy wedged Liz to his shoulder. It would be another minute before the Indians caught up. He must make every shot count. He lowered his cheek to the stock, peered at the vegetation, and stiffened.

A Karankawa was already there, his bronzed body painted for war. The man had materialized out of thin air. Acting suspicious, an arrow notched to the sinew string of his short bow, he scanned the clearing, then stooped to read the sign.

"Let him go by," James Bowie whispered.

The warrior slowly advanced, pivoting right and left. At one spot he knelt and examined tufts of trampled grass. On reaching the other side, he crisscrossed back and forth until he found where the slaves had been led off into the swamp. Then, tossing his head back, he gave voice to another of those trilling calls.

Off in the heavy growth the cry was answered. Presently, like a pack of two-legged wolves, Karankawas padded into view. Seven, eight, nine more all told, they cautiously hurried to their waiting companion.

Bowie's jaw muscles twitched. "Snake Strangler isn't with them," he whispered in disappointment. "There must be other search parties out. This one got lucky."

The Karankawas gathered together. A discussion ensued, and when it was over, two of the warriors sprinted back across the clearing.

"They'll bring the rest," Bowie said. "We can't let them." So saying, he brought his rifle to bear and felled one of them like a poled ox.

Davy shot the second messenger. The man seemed to dive face-first into the hard ground, rolled once, and was still. Davy immediately set to work reloading, while James Bowie unslung his spare rifle.

The Karankawas were not idle either. At the initial shot, they'd scattered every which way, hurtling under cover before the sound of the blast died.

"Only eight left," James said, as if that should be encouraging.

The swamp had fallen silent, as deathly still as a tomb. Where a moment ago sparrows had gaily warbled and crickets had merrily chirped, now nothing could be heard. Even the wind had died, stilling the rustle of leaves.

"We should move," Davy suggested. The Indians were

bound to know where they were, so it was crucial they change position before they were pinned down. He started to rise, but Bowie suddenly seized his arm and threw him to the side. He did not need to ask why. A quivering arrow imbedded in the log was ample explanation.

Bowie raised his rifle, but the bowman was not to be seen. "We should split up," he said urgently. "I'll draw some of them off." And in a blur he was gone, flying into a thicket as another shaft cleaved the air.

"No!" Davy objected, too late. Irate, he dashed to the right, along the tree line. Separating was a mistake in his estimation. They stood a better chance fighting side by side. But now he was on his own—with eight bloodthirsty enemies somewhere nearby.

Another trilling call gave Davy a clue to the position of the one of the Karankawas. Halting, he studied the spot intently, in vain. Aware that to stay in one place too long courted calamity, Davy glided further south, his back to the clearing.

He was glad he need not worry about enemies coming at him from behind. Then a grunt proved him wrong. Spinning, he saw the warrior he had shot rising. Blood pumped over the man's chest and pain contorted his face, but still he shuffled toward Davy with a knife poised to strike. Liz sent a ball into the warrior's ribs.

To the north Bowie's rifle spoke. Davy palmed a pistol and raced on, seeking to outflank the Karankawas and take them by surprise. They might be doing the same thing, so he was vigilant for sign of them. A dozen yards from the end of the clearing was a gap in the trees. He slanted into it, to an oak, pausing to look and listen.

Deep in the undergrowth a man groaned in agony. Davy prayed it wasn't James Bowie. Scooting to another tree, he leaned Liz against the trunk and grasped his powder horn to reload. For a fleeting instant he was distracted, but it was enough. He heard the pounding of onrushing feet and glanced up.

A Karankawa was almost on top of him. Wielding a war club, the warrior slammed into him with the force of a battering ram.

It was like the time Davy had been kicked by a mule, only worse. He smashed against the tree, bounced off, and crashed onto his side. Dazed, in torment, Davy blinked to clear his vision, and sat up. The only reason he was still alive was because the warrior had also gone down.

Davy elevated his arm, belatedly realizing the pistol was gone. He clutched at the other one, his fingers closing on empty air. He had lost both.

The Karankawa, though, still had his war club. Growling like a fierce beast, the warrior heaved into a crouch.

Davy willed his arms and legs to obey and scrambled up. His right hand slid to his tomahawk, and as the warrior charged he yanked it out and swung. Creek weapon clashed against Karankawan. Clashed, and was undamaged. They parted, circled, the warrior feinting and thrusting, testing Davy's ability.

Davy slashed low, but the man blocked it. He arced the tomahawk high, and again was thwarted. They were evenly matched, both in skill and strength. Which one of them lived and which one died depended on which one of them made the first mistake.

The Karankawa was crafty. Lunging at Davy's legs, he forced the Tennessean to jerk backwards. In doing so, Davy was momentarily off balance. And in that moment the warrior pounced, swinging viciously.

Davy countered several bruising blows. Stumbling, he righted himself, only to be clipped on the temple. His coonskin cap absorbed the brunt of it, enough so he did not lose consciousness as his legs buckled and he fell.

Howling in feral glee, the Karankawa reared above him and whisked the war club on high for a final, fatal stroke.

Chapter Five

Flavius Harris would rather be burned at the stake than split up with Davy. He hated it. Hated it, hated it, hated it. It was all he could think about as he glumly trudged at the end of the column. Matilda had always claimed that he could out-sulk a five-year-old, and he proved it now. Mired in self-pity, he paid no attention to what went on around him. When a snake slithered by, he ignored it. When a gator rose in a nearby pool and yawned wide its fearsome maw, he could not be bothered.

Flavius had cause to be upset. He had been keeping track. Ever since their gallivant began, *every time* he and Davy split up, something awful happened. Every single time. Davy could poke fun all he wanted, but Flavius was convinced there was a jinx on them. Soon another disaster would afflict them. He was sure of it.

What form it took was of no consequence. After all these weeks of grueling hardship, after surviving peril after peril, he had reached the point where it was irrelevant. Each catastrophe was as bad as the one before it.

So Flavius trudged unhappily along, waiting for impending doom to strike, and summed up his outlook by commenting to himself, "If it ain't chickens, it's feathers."

"Beg your pardon, sir?"

Flavius had forgotten about kindly Sam. "An old saying in our part of the woods."

"What does it mean, sir?"

"That if it isn't one problem, it's another." Flavius glumly regarded a blue butterfly that flitted by. "And please don't call me 'sir' anymore. I'm not your master. Matter of fact, I'm as much a slave as you are."

Sam's eyebrows arched. "You are? I've never heard of no white slaves. How can that be?"

"I'm married."

"Oh," Sam said. Then he said "Oh!" again, and pealed with delight. "I'll be a suck-egg mule! I like you, Mr. Harris. You're a humorous fellow."

"That's me, all right. A barrel of laughs." Flavius was glad to have someone to talk to, so he expanded on his notion. "When a man says, 'I do,' what he's really saying is, 'I'm yours to boss around to your heart's content.' It's always 'Yes, dear,' and 'Whatever you want, dear.' He can kiss his freedom good-bye."

Sam became serious. "You don't really believe that, do you, Mr. Harris? The right lady can make all the difference in a fella's life. I keep hopin' that Master Jimmy will find that special one for him. But he's like a bear in a shed full of honey pots. He can't make up his mind which tastes the best, so he goes from one to the other, gobblin' 'em all down. Like you were once, I bet."

Flavius had never had that problem. Females had never

fallen over themselves to share his company. Matilda was his first, his one and only.

"You must love your missus a whole lot," Sam mentioned. "Did one of those Injuns bash you on the noggin?"

"I'm serious, Mr. Harris. I saw that look in your eyes when you talked about her. You might be henpecked, but you're right fond of the hen."

"Sure," Flavius blustered. "And I can scratch my ear with my elbow." He snorted. "One of us is as dull as a meat-ax, and it isn't me."

Sam smiled. "If'n you say so. But deep down I think you're as happy as a clam. You're just too proud to own up to it. Most menfolk are. They'd rather admit they care for their hound dogs than fess up to liking their wives."

"Can you blame them? Why the Good Lord saw fit to make men and women so different is a puzzlement. You ask me, men need females like pigs need hip pockets."

"Ever think the ladies feel the same about us?" Sam pushed past a prickly bush. "My wife once told me that men are as worthless as wings on a rock. She says the only reason womenfolk put up with our shenanigans is because they can't have babies without us." Sam chuckled. "Wouldn't that be something if they could?"

"Never happen," Flavius declared. "It goes against nature. Against the laws of God. What? Do you think that one day people will pull babies out of thin air like magicians do with rabbits?" It was so preposterous, he cackled.

Suddenly the slaves in front of them halted. Flavius checked their back trail, hoping against hope for sign of Davy and James.

"What's he so mad about, you reckon?" Sam asked.

Flavius turned around. Arlo Kastner was striding toward them with both fists clenched. Through the trees Flavius spotted Sedge, waiting at the head of the line. "Something wrong?" Flavius inquired.

"Damn right there is," Arlo snapped. "Why don't you two lunkheads make a little more noise? The Karankawas might not know where we are yet." He was fit to be tied. "We can hear you clear up yonder."

"Sorry," Flavius said meekly.

Arlo sneered. "That's not good enough, bumpkin. To make sure you keep quiet, we're splittin' you up. You go up front. I'll stay here with the darkie."

Flavius resented being treated as if he were a dim-witted lout. He liked being bossed around even less. But the river rats were James's partners, so that gave them more say. More the pity, since he was growing fond of Sam's company. "I'll go," he said sullenly. Nodding at the black man, he jogged on past the two rows of slaves.

Sedge was tapping his foot. "About damn time," he groused. "You've cost us time better spent puttin' as much distance behind us as we can. I don't know about you, dullard, but I ain't partial to havin' my heart carved out and served on a spit."

"And I'm not partial to being insulted," Flavius said, his temper flaring. "So I'll thank you to keep a lid on that mouth of yours, or so help me I'll knock the bejeebers out of you."

The riverrat was genuinely surprised. "Well, well, well. The fat man is a panther in disguise. Sheathe your claws, Harris. It's the Injuns who are your enemy." He resumed their trek, holding to as rapid a clip as the shackled blacks could sustain.

Flavius thought it a shame to push the slaves so hard. But he reasoned it had to be done or none of them would escape the swamp alive. Begrudgingly, he admired the ease with which the river rat picked their route. Sedge had a knack for taking the path of least resistance, just as deer and other wild creatures would do.

The heat and muggy air took a toll. Flavius grew drowsy, and had to shake himself every now and then to stay alert. He dwelled on what Sam had said. Could it be he really did love Matilda that much? After all their spats? After she had taken a rolling pin to him more times than he could count? To say nothing of how bossy she was. He'd never mentioned it, but Matilda would make a great army sergeant. She could bellow with the best of them. And no private would dare sass her.

For over a quarter of a mile the slavers bustled on. Flavius's stomach growled repeatedly, reminding him of how ravenous he was. He was so hungry, he contemplated eating grass. Between his famished state and his musings about Matilda, he did not give Sedge another thought until the uppity river rat halted so abruptly, Flavius nearly collided with him.

"This will do nicely," Sedge said.

Flavius saw mostly water ahead. A ribbon of partially dry land, a winding, slender natural bridge, was the only means across, and it was choked with vegetation. "What will do nicely?"

"You'll see," was Sedge's perplexing reply.

Water lapped at the edges on both sides, so close that Flavius could have reached out and dipped his hands in. Gators were abundant, most of them smaller ones that would not dare attack. Most, but not all. To the north a giant reptilian back surged up out of the depths. If the visible part of the creature was any indication, it had to be as big as a horse.

Flavius made a mental note to avoid swamps from that day forth. During the Creek campaign it hadn't been quite this bad. Probably because he had been with hundreds of other men. And when an army was on the move, even alligators laid low.

Unexpectedly, Sedge asked, "Ever wanted to be rich, bumpkin?"

Annoyed that the river rat continued to insult him, Flavius responded, "Who wouldn't?" Until recently *he* hadn't, but that was beside the point.

"I do," Sedge declared. "I'd sell my own mother for five hundred dollars. My sister for a thousand."

"Why are you telling me this?" Flavius testily asked.

"Oh, to make a point." Sedge glanced at him. "How much money would it take to satisfy you, Harris?"

"I never gave it much thought."

"Well, I have. Arlo and me both." Sedge did not seem to care that the Tennessean wasn't interested. "The twelve hundred dollars Bowie agreed to pay us is more money than either of us have had at any one time in our whole lives."

You're not the only one, Flavius almost said.

"Six hundred each," Sedge rolled the sum on the tip of his tongue as if savoring sugar candy. "I can get me a room at one of the fanciest hotels in New Orleans. The kind where they change the sheets every day. Where maids in skimpy uniforms prance around speakin' French."

Flavius wouldn't mind doing that himself. Of course, Matilda would shoot him if he so much as sneaked a peek at another woman. But it might be worth it for a night of unbelievable luxury.

Sedge chattered on, more to himself. "For six hundred dollars I was willin' to risk this stinkin' swamp, the damned heathens, and whatever else I came across." He paused. "For ten times that much, I'd do just about anything. Even kill."

Ten times? Flavius performed the multiplication. It came to six thousand dollars, or exactly half of the sum James Bowie had said the sale of the blacks would bring.

For some reason, Sedge stopped. The slaves were strung out on a long straight stretch, each keeping to the center of the narrow strip. They had nowhere to go except straight ahead or straight back. "We've gone far enough, I reckon," Sedge said.

"For what?" Flavius asked.

Not responding, Sedge stepped to the edge and leaned out so he could been seen by those at the end of the line. He waved vigorously. Arlo windmilled both arms. "That's it, then," Sedge said.

"What?" Flavius said, peeved.

Sedge smirked. "Remember what I just told you? That I was willing to do *anything* for half the money these darkies will fetch?"

Flavius should have seen it coming. The river rat had dropped enough hints. But he was caught flat-footed when Sedge's rifle arced upward. The heavy stock caught him flush on the side of the head. Pain and bright pinpoints of light overwhelmed him. He felt himself stagger, and attempted to unlimber a pistol, but another blow, to the pit of his stomach, doubled him in half. Slammed backward, he tripped. Clammy wetness dampened his legs, his torso. He was vaguely conscious of being on his back in the water.

"So long, bumpkin. A couple of gators are swimmin' toward you. I'd stick around to watch them eat, but it might spoil my appetite."

Mocking laughter rang in Flavius's ears, laughter that was drowned out by a loud splash. That was the last sound he heard.

Davy Crockett had stared death in the face many times. Savage beasts, savage men, he had clashed with them time and again during his travels and always, somehow, prevailed. But in the fleeting instant before the war club descended, he knew he had come to the end of his earthly existence. He had lost his hold on the tomahawk, had no means to stop the blow from descending short of throwing an arm up. Which was exactly what he did, even though he knew the club would shatter his bones like so much dry kindling. His skull would be next.

The club swept downward. The warrior's eyes sparkled.

Then a miracle occurred. There was a flashing streak of shimmering metal. A glimmer of steel reflecting sunlight. And the hilt of a knife sprouted in the center of the Karankawa's chest. The man staggered backward, his war club shearing wide of its mark, missing the Tennessean by a cat's whisker.

Still slightly stunned from the blow to his temple, Davy rose onto his elbows. He saw the warrior blink in bewilderment at the hilt, then drop the club and grab hold to yank it out. Gurgling like an infant, the Karankawa tensed his arms. The big knife slid free. A grin spread across the man's bronzed face. As if he believed that by extracting the blade, he had insured his survival.

Popping the knife out had the same effect as popping the cork on a bottle of wine. Blood gushed from the wound like wine from a bottle's mouth, a crimson torrent that spattered the warriors, the grass, and Crockett's legs.

The Karankawa's knees buckled. He looked at Davy and his mouth moved, but he couldn't speak. His bewilderment was replaced by total shock. Feebly, he sought to stem the torrent by pressing a hand over the wound. It was akin to trying to hold back a flood with a washcloth.

Davy reclaimed his tomahawk, and rose. The Karankawa raised his face to the heavens, his lips moved as if in supplication, and he died, falling across the big knife. Davy bent to retrieve it.

"Let me." James Bowie rolled the body over, cleaned the blade as he had done before, and straightened. "I shot another. So there's only six left now."

Still too many. Davy ran to where his pistols lay, and tucked them under his belt. Squatting, he hastily began to reload Liz. "I'm obliged for saving my life," he said as the tall frontiersman cat-footed over.

"You looked as if you were a gone gosling," Bowie quipped. "Thank your Maker I've been throwing a knife since I was old enough to hold one." He had a rifle in hand, and at a sound in the brush, he turned.

No enemies appeared. Davy finished, and rose with his

back to the tree trunk. "This makes twice you've pulled my bacon out of the fire."

"It *is* becoming a habit, isn't it?" James said. "Maybe you can do the same for me some day. In the meantime, what say we learn these red pumas a thing or two about swamp fighting?" He moved eastward, darting from cover to cover.

Davy was not going to let them be separated again. He did exactly as Bowie did, his senses primed. When a Karankawa rose up out of high reeds and sighted down an arrow, he spotted the man first. "Get down!" he shouted. Simultaneously, he fired from the hip. The warrior was smashed backward, and the shaft meant for James sailed skyward to be lost amid trees to the southwest.

The tall frontiersman smiled and winked, then went on.

Davy had seldom met anyone so fearless. And he'd encountered more than his share of brave men. The land itself claimed credit for molding them. Dangerous conditions bred courage. Cowards did not last long on the frontier. Bowie's bravery was as obvious as a knight's suit of shining armor. Davy could see it in the man's eyes, in how he acted, how he handled himself in a crisis. James Bowie did not have a fearful bone in his entire body.

Friends and kin always complimented Davy on his own bravery. He had a reputation for being as stalwart as they came. And while he was flattered, he knew that there were times when he did feel fear. Just like everyone else. Times when he had been so scared, his mouth had gone dry and he had broken out in a cold sweat. Times when he had wanted to scream. So he never regarded himself as being especially brave. Especially clever, perhaps. And loyal to those who were loyal to him. But not—

Davy almost slapped himself. To let his mind drift in the heat of combat was unforgivable. Suicidal too if the Karankawas had anything to say about it. And they did, the very next second.

Five husky warriors burst from cover, one unleashing an arrow that would have taken Davy's life had he not flung himself to the right. Liz thundered, the archer toppled, and then the rest were upon them. Davy saw James Bowie slam the stock of his rifle into a Karankawa's jaw. After that he had to concentrate on his own predicament, for two of the warriors were on him in a fury, both swinging knives.

Davy flung Liz at them and the pair skipped aside, granting him the space he needed to draw both pistols. He fired as they sprang, striking the man on the right but missing the one on the left. Backpedaling, he dropped the flintlocks and resorted to his tomahawk *and* his knife. The Karankawa came at him in a whirlwind of elemental ferocity, the man's blade weaving a glittering tapestry of deadly thrusts and cuts.

Davy held his own. Standing his ground, he parried, stabbed, countered, hacked. Engrossed in simply staying alive, he did not realize the Karankawa he had just shot was still alive until a hand wrapped around his left ankle and clung fast. A glance showed the warrior had lost his weapon but not his resolve. At death's door, pouring scarlet, the Karankawa had crawled close enough to grab hold.

A meaningless act of defiance, or so it seemed until Davy jerked to the left to avoid a lancing thrust meant to disembowel him. He evaded it, although barely, his movements hampered by the anchor on his leg. Davy kicked out, but it did no good. The Karankawa's fingers were a vise.

The other warrior perceived the Tennessean's plight, and renewed his assault. Gliding to one side, he speared his blade down low.

Davy twisted to block it. Not being able to move quickly, he almost failed. As the man pumped an arm to try again, Davy threw caution to the winds and threw himself forward. He was desperate. He had to do something. So long as the one warrior clung to his leg, the outcome was inevitable unless he hampered his second foe just as he was being hampered. Arms flungs wide, he tackled the startled Karankawa, pinning the man's arms as they went down.

Davy felt a stinging sensation in his ribs. Letting go of the tomahawk, he gripped the man's knife arm to keep it at bay even as he drove his own blade up and in. Flesh gave way, and the Karankawa grunted. Davy sliced upward, the razor-sharp metal parting sinew and organs as easily as a hot knife parted wax. Warm liquid spurted over his hand and wrist. The warrior shook like a leaf in a hurricane, moaned, and sagged.

Shoving clear, Davy turned toward the one who had seized his ankle. He pumped the knife overhead, but did not carry through. The man's wide eyes were fixed in lifeless intensity on the azure ether.

Davy pried at the warrior's clenched fingers, but couldn't loosen them. James Bowie and the other two were out of sight, battling beyond a thicket. In order to reach his friend in time to help, Davy removed the Karankawa's hand the only way he could; he cut off three of the man's fingers. Once that was done, Davy tore loose and stood.

At that moment the racket behind the thicket ended. Someone mewed like a kitten. Afraid of the worst, Davy ran.

Two warriors lay at James Bowie's feet. His buckskins were ripped and grimy and sprinkled with scarlet dots. He had a cut on his right cheek, another on his leg. "They sure are scrappers, these Karankawas. I'd almost rather tangle with Comanches." He grinned. "Almost."

One other was as yet unaccounted for. Davy backed toward Bowie, saying, "I'd rather not tangle with anyone. Why don't we light a shuck while we can?"

"We might as well. The last man is probably hightailing it for Snake Strangler. We'll have forty or fifty on our tracks by this time tomorrow."

Davy noticed that Bowie's pistols were still wedged under his wide brown leather belt. "Didn't you use your guns?"

"Why bother?" James hefted the big knife. "I'm better with this."

The dead warriors testified to the truth of Bowie's assertion. Both looked as if they had been chewed up by a sawmill. Davy couldn't help but think that James Bowie must be one of the best knife fighters alive.

No arrows sought their lives as they gathered Bowie's rifles and bent their steps eastward. Bowie fairly flew. Davy blamed it on anxiety over the Karankawas. But he was wrong, as he learned when his companion paused to inspect some footprints and then blistered the air with curses.

"They're pushing harder than I told them to. In this heat it doesn't take much for a slave to shed five to ten pounds. Which will bring in less at auction."

"Arlo and Sedge are just afraid of the Karankawas," Davy speculated. "They want to get as far away as they can."

"I hope that's all it is. But say what you will about those vermin, they're not scared of anything."

"What else could it be?" Davy wanted to know. Bowie was eating up the distance in loping bounds that would do justice to an antelope. Davy had to exert himself to keep up. "Sam and Flavius are keeping an eye on them," he commented, thinking it would calm the taller man down.

Instead, Bowie went faster. A minute later, out of the blue, he said, "I refuse to lose another one. The last group was bad enough."

"How's that?" Davy replied between breaths.

Bowie's cheeks pinched tight. "I lost thirty blacks. At one time. The *only* ones I've lost out of the several hundred I've funneled into Louisiana." He was quiet for a bit. "Sam and I were alone. We had been on the go for days, and I was exhausted. Sam agreed to stand guard while I took a nap. But he fell asleep too. And when we woke up, all thirty were gone. Stolen right out from under our noses by Snake Strangler."

"He let you live?"

"Shocked me too. I think it was his way of rubbing our noses in it. Of showing he could kill us whenever he wanted if he so desired." Bowie growled like a cornered wolf. "I went after them. Tracked those devils clear to the Colorado River. But a storm came along and wiped out the trail."

"What would the Karankawas do with thirty slaves?"

"The same thing they would do with thirty whites, or thirty Pawnees, or thirty Cheyenne." Bowie was pumping his arms now. "The Karankawas aren't known as cannibals for nothing."

Eaters of human flesh. It seemed too far-fetched to Davy. In this day and age? With a modern city only a few hundred miles away? With the invention of the steam engine "promising a new age of wonder and discovery," as one newspaper put it? How could cannibals exist on the boundary of America's frontier?

"What's this?" Bowie said, stopping.

Davy could read the sign for himself. The river rats had called a halt. One of them had walked back down the line. Then Flavius—whose tracks Davy knew as well as he did his own—had gone to the head of the column. Why?

"I don't like it," James said. "Not one bit."

Not long after, Davy spied water ahead, a sprawling marshy area bisected by a strip of land no wider than his shoulders. Bowie took the lead, and had gone only a few dozen feet when up out of tall grass lunged a scarecrow figure in soaked clothes.

"Jimmy! Praise the Lord!" Sam exclaimed, and promptly collapsed.

Bowie caught his manservant and gently lowered him. A gash on Sam's forehead oozed blood and his pants were a muddy ruin. "Sam? Sam? Can you hear me?"

The black man's eyes flickered open. "Jimmy? I'm awful sorry. They took us by surprise."

"Us?" Davy said, a bolt of lightning jolting him to his

core. He scoured the swamp. "Where's Flavius, Sam? What happened to him?"

Sam grew sadder. "Two gators got him, Mr. Crockett. Ripped your poor friend to ribbons, they did."

Chapter Six

Flavius Harris had never been so scared in all his born days. Fear so potent it paralyzed him churned his vitals. Sedge's words echoed in his brain, over and over, ''A couple of gators are swimmin' toward you.'' The hideous creatures were going to eat him! Gobble him up in great grisly chunks! And there was nothing he could do about it!

Then someone else drowned out the river rat. Impossibly, he heard Davy yelling. Yelling something Davy had said plenty of times: ''Where there's life, there's hope! So long as you're alive, *never* give up!''

And a tiny voice Flavius recognized as his own shrilly screamed, *''Don't just lie there! Do something!''*

Flavius raised his head and blinked water from his eyes. He saw Sedge smirking evilly. Twisting, he spotted an alligator to his right, its back cleaving the water like the prow of a canoe. To the left was a second, even larger, brute. They seemed to be in a race to see which would get to take the first bite.

Flavius had lost Matilda when he fell. He still had his pistols, but both were soaked and liable to misfire. As for his knife, he dismissed it as worthless. He might as well throw spitballs.

Instinct took over where reason failed. The smaller of the alligators reached him a fraction of an instant before the other. It started to open its mouth wide. And Flavius, at the sight of its terrible teeth, sucked air into his lungs and flung himself downward, diving for the bottom. He had a vague idea that if he could swim *under* the beast, he could gain a few precious moments of life. A sharp tug on his hunting shirt almost upended him. Then he was free, but only for a second.

A blow to the small of his back smashed him into clinging muck. It was as if a tree had fallen on him. Only this tree had four rending limbs and rapier claws. The gator tore at his shoulders, at his hips. Mud seeped up pinto Flavius's nostrils, into his eyes. He could not see a thing. The pressure grew worse, tremendously worse, his spine and ribs shrieking in protest.

Flavius tried to brace both hands and push, but he could not find a purchase. His fingers sank deeper into the muck. Frantic, he wrenched to the right. There was a ripping sensation along his back. Suddenly he was loose, and like an oversized crab he scuttled swiftly away, listening to the water roil behind him. Loud splashing buffeted his ears.

Certain the gators were hunting for him, Flavius glanced back. Two mighty tails whipped the water in a frenzy. Huge bodies rolled over and over. Incredibly, neither of the alligators were interested in him. Not knowing what to make of it, his lungs aching, Flavius swam on. Staying below the surface to avoid detection, he pumped his arms again and again. Only when his lungs were fit to burst did he arch upward.

He was sixty feet from where he had fallen in. The gators were locked in combat, their monstrous forms agitating the water into a bubbling foam. From the jaw of the smaller dangled part of his hunting shirt, impaled on several teeth.

As for Sedge, the river rat was watching in amusement. "Stupid brutes!" he bantered. "Why fight? That fat fool has enough meat on him for the both of you, and ten just like you besides."

Flavius ducked under and continued to swim. Burning rage lent him strength. Always the most peaceable of souls, he rarely harbored ill will toward anyone. But he sorely wanted to wring the river rat's skinny neck! Or to shoot Sedge so full of holes, he'd look like a sieve! The riverman and his partner were cold-blooded fiends. If ever someone deserved to die, it was them!

Again Flavius surfaced. He had doubled the distance. Ahead, against the bank, grew a thick patch of reeds. A prime place for snakes. Flavius swam into it anyway and lowered both legs. He could stand, but he did not climb out. Not yet. Shivering more from his narrow escape than the coolness of the water, he wrapped his arms across his chest and waited.

Presently, a shout rang out. Soon the tramp of feet sounded. Peering up through the reeds, Flavius saw Sedge hiking merrily along. The river rat was as happy as a lark, whistling to himself. Next came the glum slaves, trudging noisily, their chains clanking and rattling. Last, Arlo Kastner strolled by, beaming like someone who had just won a turkey shoot.

Small wonder. The river rats had the blacks all to themselves now. They'd find a buyer of their own and reap the profits, have enough money to last a lifetime if they didn't squander it. More than likely, they would split it and make themselves scarce, maybe head back East so James couldn't find them.

Flavius did not move until the slavers were out of sight. Pushing reeds aside, he took a step, only to freeze when a sinuous shape wound off among the stems. Steeling himself, he scrambled onto solid ground and sank onto his knees. Relief and gratitude poured through him. By the grace of the Almighty, he was alive. It was a miracle.

If it was the last thing he ever did, Flavius vowed, he would make the river rats pay. He would wait for Davy and James to return, then Sam and he would—*Sam! What had happened to him? Sam hadn't been with the others when they marched past*. Filled with alarm, Flavius heaved erect and hurried back along the trail. He almost called out Sam's name, but thought better of it; the slavers might hear.

A commotion in the water brought him to a halt. The alligators were still there. Or rather, one of them was. The bigger beast was *eating* the smaller. No one had ever told Flavius they did such a thing. Evidently human beings weren't the only cannibals. The smaller gator's belly had been ripped open, spilling its guts, which the larger beast chewed on with reptilian gusto.

Flavius began to sidle past, one slow step at a time. He was shocked to discover his rifle in the grass at the water's edge. It made no sense to him for the river rats to leave a perfectly good rifle behind, until he recollected both already had two rifles apiece. One more would be an unnecessary extra burden.

Flavius took a step toward his gun, then imitated a tree. The big alligator had stopped chewing and was staring at him with what Flavius could only describe as a wicked gleam in its eyes. Less than ten feet away, it could reach him unbelievably quickly if it elected. Flavius swallowed hard, slowly tucked at the knees, and extended his right hand.

The gator stirred. Lifting its snout, it cocked its head as if to better study him. Then, apparently deciding he was no threat, it resumed chomping and tearing at its rival.

Flavius snatched Matilda and bolted. He remembered approximately where Arlo and Sam had been standing when the river rats struck, and he scoured the vicinity, finding crumpled grass and a scarlet smear but no body. "Sam?" he said softly.

Out in the water several other gators milled. Flavius guessed that Arlo had slain the black man, then thrown the body in to dispose of the evidence.

"Oh, Sam," Flavius said sorrowfully. He had liked the man. It would have been nice to sit down over a pitcher of ale and swap stories sometime.

His fury returned, with a vengeance. The river rats must be held to account! Pivoting, he gave chase, jogging past the big gator with nary a glance. Somehow, he would stop them. Somehow, he would make them pay for their base treachery and the foul murder.

Flavius thought about staying put until Davy and James caught up. But he didn't know how long that would be. Hours maybe, and he didn't fancy being all alone all that while. Already, the enormity of the swamp gnawed at his nerves. On all sides were water and rank growth, crawling with creatures of every kind, creatures that would as soon kill him as look at him.

Flavius ran faster. The tracks were clearly defined in the soft soil. It didn't take a Davy Crockett to follow them. So it was not all that long before Flavius glimpsed movement in the distance and distinguished Arlo's slender frame. Flavius slowed, content to dog them for the time being, until he concocted a plan of action.

Picking them off from hiding had merit. The only drawback was that Flavius had to wait for nightfall, when they made camp, so the two cutthroats would be together.

Flavius prayed that Davy and James were all right. On his own, he stood as much chance of making it through the swamp as a wingless goose did of making it south for the winter. The blacks would be no help. The swamp was as foreign to them as it was to him. More so, since they were strangers in a strange land, a land they did not want to be in. A land they had been dragged to against their will.

Flavius could not imagine how they must feel. Frightened,

lost, bitter, resentful. Sad too, he reckoned. Inexpressibly sad. Everyone and everything they loved were thousands of miles away. Lost to them for all time. They were like flowers ripped out by the roots and cast into the wind. No one should have to go through the nightmare they were enduring.

Then and there, Flavius made up his mind he was against slavery and would be for as long as he lived. It was inhuman, treating people as if they were animals. No, *less* than animals. Horses and cows weren't forced to go around shackled to one another, were they?

A *crack-crack-crack* drew Flavius's gaze to the slavers. He had to sneak closer to learn the cause. One of the slaves in the second bunch, an older man whose sorrow perpetually bent his shoulders, was on his knees with his head bowed. Either he had collapsed, or he'd simply refused to go on. Whichever the case, it incensed Arlo Kastner. The river rat was applying a whip to the old man's back, the lash biting deep.

"On your feet, you damn darkie!" Arlo fumed. "If you don't, I'll peel you like an onion. So help me, God!"

The old man didn't so much as flinch. He absorbed the punishment silently, almost as if he didn't feel the sting of the rawhide. The other slaves were aghast, but there was little they could do.

Arlo might have gone on beating the old man until the black was a quivering wreck, but at that juncture Sedge appeared, waving his arms and saying, "What in hell do you think you're doing? Tryin' to kill him?"

"If I have to!" Arlo responded, pausing for breath. His face was slick and his chest rose and fell with each breath.

"Mighty smart of you," Sedge said sarcastically. "Let a temper tantrum cost us six or seven hundred dollars. Why don't you shoot a few more while you're at it?"

Arlo did not appreciate his companion's humor. "What

else would you have me do? Beg him to get his lazy ass on the move?''

"No. There's an easier way. All you have to do is *think*," Sedge said, tapping his temple. Then, striding to a young woman who cringed in terror, he leveled a rifle and jammed the muzzle into her stomach. Sneering at the old man, he stated, "I know you don't savvy a lick of English, you bastard. But you'll savvy this. Get on your feet and move out or I'll blow a hole in this bitch.''

The old man stared at the woman. She said something in an unknown tongue, and the old man shook his head. Tears came into her eyes as he stiffly rose, giving the chain a shake to loosen the shackle a trifle. Squaring his bloody shoulders, he faced Sedge, and motioned to show he was ready to comply.

Sedge snickered. Lowering his rifle, he crowed, "There. See, Arlo? It's not so hard when you use your brain. Darkies can't hold a candle to white folks when it comes to smarts. You ought to know that.''

Kastner was coiling the whip. "What I know is that I don't much like being treated like a simpleton. What would you have done if the old geezer didn't listen? Shoot her and him both? We'd lose twice as much money.''

"Nah. These darkies stick up for one another," Sedge said. "They have to. It's how they survive." He headed forward. "Next time one acts up, give a holler. I'll show you how to deal with 'em.''

From his place of concealment, Flavius saw Arlo glare at Sedge's retreating back, and heard Arlo growl when Sedge was beyond earshot, "I'll show *you*, you smug jackass. I'm tired of your attitude. More and more I like the idea of how nice it would be to have *all* the money, not just half.''

So the river rats were having a falling out, Flavius mused. He wished there were some means of turning it to his advantage. They continued on, and so did he, though not for very long. Ten minutes later Sedge gave a whoop, bringing the blacks to a halt. Arlo hastened to the front to find out why.

Flavius bided his time. The ruffians were bound to hurry on; they knew that Davy and James would be after them. Mystified, he watched the pair climb a short slope to what appeared to be a low hillock that bordered the game trail. Sedge pointed at several spots, and Arlo nodded as if excited by whatever Sedge was proposing.

Flavius was eager to overhear, but he didn't relish venturing into the water to sneak around. The problem was solved when the slavers herded their captives to the base of the slope, and had the blacks pick up long branches and sharp stones and whatever else could be used as implements. Arraying ten at one point and the other ten at another, Sedge, through gestures, directed them to dig.

More mystified then ever, Flavius snuck as near as he dared. Arlo was at the bottom of the slope, back toward him, while the other cutthroat was at the top, pacing back and forth.

"Dig faster!" Sedge goaded. "So help me, if Bowie and Crockett show up before you're done, I'll kill as many of you as I can out of sheer spite!"

Arlo was all smiles. "Those two will never catch us now. This brainstorm of yours is brilliant, partner. It will wipe out our tracks for hundreds of feet. By the time Bowie picks up our scent again, we'll be too far ahead." He chortled. "And here I thought you were all mouth!"

"Oh?" Sedge said.

"You have me convinced," Arlo said. "I admit you're smarter than me. Just don't let it give you a swelled head."

Flavius witnessed something Arlo didn't. Sedge's features rippled, becoming a mask of pure resentment. The expression lasted fleeting seconds; then Sedge adopted an oily smile instead. "Hell, I've been tellin' you that for ages. Glad to hear you finally agree."

The black men and women were scooping out prodigious amounts of soft earth and flinging it to either side. The reason eluded Flavius, until one of the slaves cried out and pointed at a trickle of water seeping from the hole they were excavating.

With a start, Flavius realized the hillock was really a slightly elevated basin. A large pool must be on the other side of that slope. Once the wall crumbled, water would gush out, flowing over the swamp for quite a ways, a minor flood that would obliterate tracks and trail alike. It *was* brilliant.

Another black yelled. More water seeped through, bearing globs of earth, eating at the dirt like acid. Arlo had the slaves move to the north of the slope. Sedge, descending, examined their handiwork, and commanded ten to apply themselves where the slope was weakest. In no time whole sections were being expelled by gushing torrents.

Almost too late, Sedge ordered the diggers to safety. The slope was eroding at a fantastic rate. Violent spray shot from it at several points.

Viewing the watery onslaught was like watching a damn buckle. Flavius was enthralled. Abruptly, with a turbulent rending and a sibilant hiss, half the slope shattered and was borne toward the trail by a foaming wave over six feet high.

Only then did Flavius awaken to the danger he was in. The water was rushing toward *him,* and if he broke into the open to flee, the river rats would spy him and open fire. Yet what else could he do?

Roaring like the Biblical Leviathan, a solid frothing wall bore down on him with the destructive force of a runaway steam engine.

"There, Mr. Crockett. Right about there is where I saw your friend fall in." Sam nodded. "Sedge gave him a fierce wallop. About split his skull open, it looked like. That's when he fell, and two gators were on him like tomcats on a mouse."

Davy moved into the water. A wide area was discolored, darker than it should be, and bits and pieces of flesh bobbed like tiny corks. Bile rose in his throat.

"I saw one of the gators bite down," Sam detailed. "Then I started to run to help, but Arlo hit me. I must have blacked out. When I came to, I was in the water my own self, and a gator was swimming toward me. I crawled into the weeds and lay there for I don't know how long, too weak to get up. I'd lost a lot of blood."

"Which is what saved your life," James Bowie commented. "Arlo mistook you for dead, or he'd have finished you off."

"I'm terribly sorry about Flavius," Sam told the Irishman. "He was a sweet, kindly fella. Powerful fond of talking about food, but there are worse flaws."

It was meant to cheer Davy a trifle, but he was too distraught. *Not Flavius!* he thought, wading deeper. The level rose to his knees.

"I wouldn't were I you, sir," Sam warned. "Those monsters are still around. And they're like hogs. They never get enough."

"He's right," Bowie said. "Get out of there."

Davy refused. He had to be sure. He had to know beyond any shadow of a doubt that his best friend was gone, gone forever. A pale object bobbed nearby, an object remarkably like a human forearm. Loathe to touch it, Davy poked it with Liz's stock, turning it over. It was a limb, all right, but it belonged to an alligator.

Bowie had moved nearer to cover him. "The gators must have fought over the body. They do that sometimes."

"But there's no sign of *him*," Davy said. Hardly were the words out of his mouth when he saw something else floating a few yards further out. Thrusting the stock underneath, he lifted a soaked, jagged strip of buckskin into the sunlight.

"Damn!" Bowie swore.

"I'm truly sorry," Sam reiterated.

Davy searched for more strips, but there were none. He roved to the right and left, the water rising almost to his hips. To his pistols. He didn't care. All he could think of was Flavius, ripped into a hundred bits, and how it was all his own fault for dragging Flavius on this latest gallivant.

"Come back!" James said. "What are you trying to prove? You'll only get yourself killed, Tennessee."

What was *he trying to prove?* Davy asked himself. The alligator had likely dragged the rest of Flavius off to its lair. He couldn't give his friend a decent burial. Couldn't even kill the gator. All he could do was mourn. His eyes moistened and his throat constricted, and he was on the verge of sobbing when he remembered who bore even more of the blame. "Arlo and Sedge," he said aloud.

Bowie had stepped into the water. "What about them? If we push, maybe we can catch up before dark. You do want to see justice done, don't you?"

Davy had never wanted anything more. Wading onto shore, he wrung the buckskin, neatly folded it, and slid it into his leather pouch. He would take the keepsake to Tennessee. The least he could do was have a formal ceremony, with a coffin, a minister, and flowers. He owed that much to Flavius. And to Matilda, who was bound to take the news hard. For all her carping, despite the countless tongue-lashings she had given Flavius, she cared as deeply for her husband as any woman alive. "I'm ready."

Bowie's long legs ate up the distance. It was soon obvious, however, that Sam was not sufficiently recovered to hold to the pace Bowie set. They stopped twice in fifteen minutes, Davy chafing at each delay. His impatience was as plain as the nose on his face. "Maybe you should go on ahead," James proposed. "Sam and I will come as fast as we can."

"Will you be safe?" Davy asked, thinking of the Karankawas.

"Safer than you'll be," Bowie said. "A man alone is easy pickings." He paused. "You should overtake them before nightfall. But if you don't, pick as high a spot as you can find and build a fire so snakes and the like will let you be."

Davy did not waste another moment. Touching a finger to his coonskin cap, he was off, jogging at a reckless speed. The position of the sun told him it was past four, but he was still supremely confident. It was the middle of the summer. Sunset didn't occur until eight o'clock. That gave him plenty of time. The river rats had an hour's lead, maybe slightly more. Nowhere near enough. He would have Arlo and Sedge in his rifle sights before night fell.

Within an hour, Davy's legs were sore, his muscles taut. He should stop and rest a spell, but he refused. He would when Flavius's killers had been punished, not before.

It was about five-thirty when the Tennessean came to a barren strip of soft earth the slavers had crossed. He was halfway across when a distinct set of footprints brought him up short in amazement. They were overlaid on top of the tracks made by the river rats and the blacks. Moccasin prints, these were. Squatting, he ran a finger along the edge and noted the width and depth.

Only one person could have made them. A person who was as much Davy's brother as his own kin. "I wish I may be shot if these aren't his," he said to himself.

But they couldn't be.

Davy had the strip of buckskin in his pouch to prove it. He had Sam's testimony and the evidence of his own eyes. He compared the tracks to his own, studied them from various angles, and held to his opinion.

"Flavius!"

Renewed vigor animated Davy as he took up the pursuit. Somehow his friend had survived and was trailing the slavers on his own. That in itself was cause for distress. Flavius was a fairly competent woodsman and a fair hand with a rifle, but he was no match for two merciless vermin like Sedge and Arlo.

More time passed on turtle's feet. Davy found where the slavers had briefly stopped, which was encouraging. Every delay on their part worked in his favor. He grew weary, but would not slow down.

Guilt racked him. He had not been there when Flavius needed him; he would not make the same mistake twice.

Then a strange thing happened.

The terrain became monotonous marsh. For quite a while Davy had been flying along a winding game trail the slavers had used. He expected to come on them at any moment. Rounding a bend, he was up to his ankles in muddy water before he realized the trail had ended with bewildering suddenness. Stopping, he backpedaled onto dry ground and scrutinized the area ahead.

Something was amiss. Water stretched for hundreds of yards to the north and south and west, yet there was no indication the river rats had gone around. What then? Davy couldn't see them wading across, not at the risk of losing valuable slaves to marauding gators. Where else had they gone then? Had they vanished into thin air?

Davy slanted to the right, slowing when another peculiar fact struck him. For scores of yards to the east, bushes and trees poked up out of the water as if they had recently sprouted. Which was impossible. And if they had been there a good long while, the water, plainly, *had not*.

Baffled, Davy tramped to the south a short distance, then an equal distance to the north. Beyond certain points the water was clear. As improbable as it seemed, an upheaval of some kind—a flood caused by God knows what—had inundated a wide dry tract. Including the slavers' trail.

What could have caused it? was the big question. Rain had not fallen in days—in weeks. And floods did not occur on their own. Something had to trigger them.

Davy returned to the trail, debated, and waded on out. Lady Luck willing, he would pick up the tracks again on the other side. Provided the slavers had gone straight on. He counted his steps, and at 210 he stepped onto dry terra firma again. However, a hasty survey filled him with apprehension.

No footprints were anywhere to be seen. Davy glanced at the blazing orb in the western sky, well on its downward arc, and indulged in a bout of lurid swearing. The unthinkable had happened. Despite his best efforts, despite spurring himself to exhaustion, he was worse off now than when he'd started.

He had lost the trail.

Chapter Seven

Flavius Harris started to back away from the onrushing wall of roiling water, and tripped. He tried to rise, but it was on him before he could. A liquid battering ram slammed into his side, bowling him over. He tumbled head over heels, barely able to retain his grip on Matilda. A tremendous hissing filled his ears. Something hard hit his leg. Something else, long and sinuous, wriggled against his arm and was gone.

Flavius tried to resist the tide, but it was hopeless. It was like being buffeted by a giant's hand. He could no more resist the water's pull than he could withstand a buffalo stampede. Trees shot past him. Crumpled brush whirled into a murky void. Animals flitted in front of his eyes; frogs, salamander, snakes, and more. Once, a small gator zipped on by, trail thrashing.

Flavius had neglected to suck in a deep breath before the wave engulfed him. He needed to reach the surface, but he did not know which direction to go. Dizzy, disoriented, he struggled to slow himself down. He might as well have attempted to stem the Mississippi's flow.

A jarring impact did what Flavius was unable to do on his own. He smashed into a tree, the impact whooshing what little air he had left from his lungs. His left arm happened to loop around the trunk, and he clung on for dear life.

His chest was fit to explode. His vision dimmed. Soon, whether he wanted to or not, he must gasp for air that was not there.

The end was near.

Then the pressure slackened. The water stopped pummeling him. He straightened, astonished when his head broke clear. He could breathe again.

Suddenly, to his left, a huge alligator appeared. Its enormous head swung from side to side, and it snorted just like a bull. It was mad as hell and searching for something to take out its wrath on.

Flavius did not so much as twitch. When the reptile turned and paddled furiously away, he straightened. The water level was dropping rapidly. His feet settled on firm ground and he stood.

Around him living things writhed and flopped and squirmed. Tadpoles, fish, a bullfrog, even a turtle. To the west the white froth receded as the wave diminished. To the east, the last of the slaves entered a strip of verdant growth. Arlo Kastner was at the rear, and he never bothered to glance back.

Flavius suppressed an urge to whoop for joy. Leaning against the ground, he checked Matilda and the pistols. Both were hopelessly soaked, and had to be dried and reloaded. The only thing was, if he took the time, the river rats might get away. And he could ill afford to lose them.

Muddy water lapped against his legs as he waded toward the woods. He stepped over a black snake, avoided a middling-sized gator.

The slavers were traveling to the northwest this time. Strange, since New Orleans was to the east, but he figured they knew the swamp better than he did. He stayed well enough behind to avoid being detected.

It disturbed him that the sun would set in a couple of hours. He never had liked the dark much, even as a little boy. Many a night he had cowered under the blankets, convinced a demon lurked under the bed or was hiding in his closet. On occasion, he'd sworn he could see blazing red eyes glare at him from corners of the room. He even gave the demon a name: Old Scratch.

His grandmother—bless her soul—had been partly to blame. She'd had a fondness for telling scary stories. And one of her favorites involved Scratch, a spawn of the Pit who, Grandma claimed, delighted in stealing bad children and whisking them down to the nether regions, there to toil in infernal flames forever more.

Flavius had practically been a grown man before he stopped believing in Old Scratch. He knew the demon was the product of his granny's tall tales, yet on thunderous, stormy nights, when he lay awake beside Matilda, sometimes he glimpsed those blazing red eyes in the shadows, and he would snuggle closer to his snoring wife.

Over an hour had gone by when it dawned on Flavius that he had made a mistake. The torrent of water had undoubtedly flooded a considerable portion of the trail, wiping out their tracks. Davy would have to search and search to find where they had gone on. It would have helped his friend immensely if Flavius had thought to blaze trees to mark the route they were taking.

"Damn me for a fool," Flavius said under his breath.

It was not his only oversight. For moments later, when he hopped over a log, a large snake with curved fangs as long as his thumb darted out from under it and bit at him. By sheer coincidence, he had started to lower Liz, and the snake mistook the stock for part of his body and slashed at the wood instead. Startled, Flavius reversed his grip, fixed a hasty bead on the scurrying serpent, flicked the hammer back, and squeezed the trigger.

Nothing happened. There was a *click*, and that was it. The rifle had misfired, justifiably so, since he had forgotten to dry it and reload. The same with his pistols. It scared him to think he had been traipsing through the swamp with no means to protect himself other than his knife.

Now he was in a quandary. To reload, he must stop, and if he stopped, the slavers would gain ground. Yet it had to be done. Halting, he watched the line of figures fade into the vegetation; then he yanked out the ramrod and went to work.

The task took much longer than Flavius anticipated. The useless wet powder had to be removed, a painstaking process since much of it clung to the insides of the barrels. He persevered, though, and was rewarded with three primed weapons and restored confidence.

Shouldering Liz, Flavius hastened after the slavers. The sun sat balanced on the western rim of the world. Shadows were long and ominous.

At any moment Flavius would spot them. All he need do was wait until the river rats let down their guard, then end it. Sam would be avenged. The blacks would be rescued.

Or would they? Flavius frowned. Saving the slaves from Sedge and Arlo would accomplish little. James would still sell them in New Orleans. They would still spend the rest of their earthly days toiling on a plantation somewhere.

What else then? Should he free them? Unfasten their shackles and let them go? Flavius pondered heavily. *Where* could they go if he did? It wasn't as if they could waltz onto a ship and book return passage to Africa. Nor could they make a go of it on their own. They had no money, no clothing to speak of. Hell, they didn't even know English. They would be branded as runaways wherever they went, and put on the auction block.

Flavius wondered if they could live in the wild. Not in the swamp, like the Karankawas, but off on the prairie somewhere, like the Pawnees and the Osage. Davy might even help relocate them.

Flavius was getting ahead of himself. His grand plan overlooked a crucial element. James would hardly be willing to give them up without a fight. Not when they were worth twelve thousand dollars.

Deep in thought, Flavius forged on. The undergrowth grew murky and somber, the trees taking on the aspect of inky sentinels. An owl hooted, a harbinger of night. He rose onto his toes to try and spot the slavers' fire.

Where could they have gotten to? Flavius stopped to scour the ground, and was treated to a shock. There were no footprints. He had drifted off the trail! He spun and ran back, anxious to find it again.

The sun was gone. With it, the last vestige of light faded. Twilight swooped in, blanketing everything in deepening shades of gray.

Flavius thought to climb a tree. The slavers were bound to have a camp nearby. It would serve as a beacon, guiding him through the night. But when he clambered into a fork, mocking darkness taunted him. Either they had not built their fire yet—or he was so far behind, he couldn't see it.

"Oh, God. I'm lost."

Flavius began to climb down, then changed his mind. Night was falling. Blundering about in pitch darkness did not appeal to him. Predators would be on the prowl. Snakes and gators would be out in greater numbers. The safest place to be was exactly where he was, up a tree.

The fork was uncomfortably small, but he could make do. To insure he wouldn't fall out, he tucked his pistols and knife under his pants and removed his wide belt, which he looped around a narrow limb and secured around his midriff.

Sleep was a long time coming. Flavius was hungry enough to eat a moose raw, and his stomach reminded him of it by snarling noisily often.

A spectacular starry spectacle blossomed overhead, but he was too depressed to give it more than a brief survey.

During daylight hours the swamp was rife with the songs of birds and the droning of insects, punctuated by the occasional bellow of a gator or the bleat of deer. A man got accustomed to it after a while.

But the daylight sounds were nothing in comparison to those at night. Early on, frogs croaked in a throaty chorus that swelled in volume as time went by. Crickets joined in. Gators bellowed without cease. Birds added to the din, but not by warbling. The new birdcalls were strident screeches, the death throes of those pounced on by bobcats and sundry other meat-eaters. Other, less identifiable sounds were mixed in screams, groans, and grunts galore, enough to set a grown man's teeth to chattering if he wasn't careful.

Flavius wrapped his arms tight across his chest and thanked his Maker it wasn't worse. That was when the heavy *thud* of enormous feet rose from below. Looking down, he saw a vague shape, a four-legged creature that walked in a circle and sniffed the air. A bear was his initial guess. But no bear alive had such short rear legs in relation to the front. The thing had detected his scent, but couldn't pinpoint where he was, and it was peeved.

Flavius did not like to dwell on the outcome if it did. He was glad when another animal passed by, creating a racket in the brush. Growling hideously, the thing under the tree lumbered off after it.

Allowing himself the luxury of breathing again, Flavius hooked a leg over a limb as added insurance he wouldn't fall. He didn't anticipate falling asleep for quite some time, so he

was surprised when he woke with a start and saw by the stars
that he had slumbered for a couple of hours.

Flavius figured he had awakened of his own accord, but a
nauseating stench proved him wrong. He sniffed, and almost
gagged. *A skunk!* he thought, scouring the area. No white
stripes were in his vicinity. But he did see a man-shaped form
crouched beside a thicket—unless his imagination was playing tricks on him. As he watched, the figure rose, shuffled in
an unnatural gait to the base of the tree, and looked up.

It knew he was there. Flavius set eyes on a hairy face that
would do justice to a monkey. Which was preposterous. Apes
were not found in North America. Or were they? *So this was
what the Texicans meant by a three-toed skunk ape,* he reflected. Covering his nose and mouth, he waited for the abom-
ination to drift elsewhere.

Eventually, the creature did. Flavius could not relax for
hours afterward, and it was during the second hour, when his
eyelids were growing leaden, that guttural voices announced
he had new visitors. Only these were *human*.

The first one strode by within a dozen feet of the tree, a
tall, lean Indian in a short loincloth. The man paused, studied
the benighted landscape to the east, then gestured with a war
club. One by one, eight others tramped past.

Flavius supposed they were Karankawas, but the more he
saw, the more he doubted it. They were much taller, nowhere
near as brawny, with spindly arms and legs, in contrast to the
muscular limbs of Snake Strangler's people. They walked
with a peculiar shuffling gait reminiscent of the skunk ape.
And unkempt black manes hung past their shoulders.

Flavius had been afeared of tangling with the Karankawas,
but no more so than he would be of Comanches or the Sioux.
The warriors below, though, filled him with unspeakable
dread. With an unreasoning fear that chilled him to the mar-
row and made him want to leap down and race off into the
night.

Resisting, Flavius stayed where he was, his every nerve jangling. The last time he had felt like this was when a pack of famished wolves surrounded Davy and him out on the prairie. He had the same conviction now, that a single wrong move on his part would prove fatal.

The last warrior was gone. Flavius relaxed muscles he had not realized were taut, and leaned back. This was what it would be like every night thereafter, he mused, unless he met up with Davy again. He gazed westward, praying to spot a fire. But it was the same old story.

The rest of the night was uneventful. Flavius dozed in fitful spurts.

Shrieking jays trumpeted the dawn. The Tennessean snapped his head up, befuddled, forgetting where he was, and cried out when he started to pitch forward. The belt held, and the fright restored his senses. He unfastened himself, wrapped the belt around his waist where it belonged, replaced the pistols, and started down.

A thin scream wavered in the distance. Flavius froze, perplexed. When it was repeated, he pegged the direction it came from as northwest. The same direction the slavers had taken. Sedge or Arlo, he supposed, tormenting one of the blacks. He willed his stiff joints to function, and dashed into the undergrowth.

A rifle cracked, crisp and clear. The screaming did not stop. Seconds more and a second rifle boomed.

A slave wasn't being beaten. The slavers were under attack. Half a mile away, Flavius estimated. He ran flat out, doing his best to avoid briars and branches. What he would do when he got there remained to be seen.

The swamp had fallen totally silent. Flavius could hear his labored breathing, could hear the *thump-thump-thump* of his soles striking the ground. And soon he heard a new element, the crash of brush as something plowed through it, coming right toward him.

Halting, Flavius crouched and trained Matilda on a small clearing. Whatever was approaching must cross it to reach him. If it was an Indian, he would shoot on sight. If it was a black, he would demonstrate he was peaceable. Those were the two best possibilities. It never occurred to him that it might be one of the river rats. Yet that was exactly what it turned out to be.

Arlo Kastner barreled through a thicket into the clearing, and stopped to glance over a shoulder. He had no rifle, no pistol. His shirt was ripped, his pants leg torn from the knee to the hip, and his face battered and bruised. Mewing like a kitten, he resumed his flight.

Flavius was dumfounded. The hardened cutthroat's features reflected pure panic. Flavius couldn't recollect ever seeing anyone so scared. Pale as a sheet, eyes as wide as saucers, mouth agape, Kastner took several more steps, then spied him.

"You!"

"Put your hands in the air and don't move," Flavius directed.

The river rat kept coming. "No! No! We have to get out of here! Now!"

Flavius held Matilda steady. "I won't say it again," he warned. "Raise your arms and stand still."

Arlo stopped, but he was none too pleased. "Listen to me!" he pleaded. "I'm the only one who got away! But they must be on my trail! We can't dally. They'll track me down, I'm sure."

"Who?"

"Indians," Arlo answered, his panic increasing. "Savages the likes of which I've never set eyes on before! Unholy devils!"

"Not Karankawas?"

The slaver wrung his hands. "I wish to hell they had been! You should have seen them! Hairy as buffalo! And the way

98

they moved!'' Licking his lips, he pleaded, ''Please! I'm beggin' you! Take me wherever you want, just so we leave while we can!''

This was a switch, Flavius noted. Yet Kastner acted completely sincere. ''Where's your friend?'' Flavius demanded. ''And the rest of the blacks? Don't tell me you ran out on them?''

''I had no choice!'' Arlo lamented. ''They were on us before Sedge or me could do a thing. Four of 'em grabbed me and stripped me of my guns. But Sedge had his rifles handy. He shot two of them. That was when I made my escape.''

''You deserted your own friend?''

The river rat did not seem to hear. ''Their eyes! You should have seen their eyes! All red-rimmed! And dark. So dark, like an animal's.'' Choking his words off, he quaked. ''Please! ''Please! I don't want to die! We must go!''

Flavius hesitated. Helping the slaves was the important thing, but the cutthroat's raw fear was contagious. What kind of Indians were these that they could inspire such terror in an iron-hearted killer?

A piercing howl confirmed they were indeed after Kastner, who whined. Another howl, to the south, answered the first.

''Stick with me,'' Flavius said, beckoning.

The river rat ran to him, and together they thrust into a dense thicket and crouched. Arlo's hands were shaking uncontrollably. Flavius turned to tell him to be still, and saw the slaver's eyes bulge.

One of the Indians had appeared. Across the clearing, framed by a backdrop of vines and leaves, he studied the clearing before venturing into the open.

Flavius's skin crawled. The previous night he had been struck by how eerily unnerving the warriors were. In the pale glow of a new dawn, the eerie aspect was magnified. Shaggy hair framed a brutish face dominated by darkling eyes and a leonine nose. Thick lips framed a cruel mouth. The man was practically skin and bones, yet bones packed with sinew. Short, curly hair covered his chest and legs, and had even sprouted on his cheeks and chin. From the top of his only weapon, a curved war club, jutted a thick spike, rendering it twice as deadly.

The warrior was definitely not a Karankawa.

Texicans had told Flavius and Davy the swamp was home to other tribes, including some who'd had little or no contact with whites. Rumor had it that deep in the festering interior dwelled Indians more fierce than the notorious Apaches. Cut off from the rest of the world, the lost tribes had one trait in common. They shared a fondness for human flesh.

Arlo Kastner was rigid with fear. Flavius was worried the river rat would bolt and give them away, but Arlo stayed as still as a statue as the warrior advanced to the middle of the clearing and hunkered down to run his fingers over the ground. Throwing back his head, the man voiced a wolfish howl. A signal that elicited a reply.

Presently, a second warrior glided out of the greenery. The pair barked at one another in a tongue as unlike human speech as any Flavius ever heard. They moved toward the thicket, and Flavius gripped a pistol.

Arlo's eyes were on the verge of rolling up into his head. He was close to fainting.

Discovery was imminent. Then, to the east, a series of howls had a helpful effect. The pair of hulking brute-men turned and slogged back the way they had come, making no more noise than did the wind.

Kastner collapsed with a groan. Lying on his left side, he shook from head to toe, his teeth chattering, broken in soul and mind if not in body. ''Oh, God. Oh, God. Oh, God,'' he said softly.

Flavius would rather shoot the river rat than help him, but he gave Arlo's shoulder a squeeze. ''Get a hold of yourself. You're safe now.''

"No, no, no. No one is ever safe from *them*."

"What tribe do they belong to?" Flavius whispered.

"Who knows? Who cares?" Arlo covered his face and curled into a fetal position. "Leave me, Tennessee. I'm in no shape to go anywhere for a spell. We have a better chance if we split up anyhow."

Suspicion flared. Flavius shook Kastner roughly. "You're not getting shed of me that easily, mister. We're going to do what we can for those black folks, and after that I'll decide what to do with you."

Arlo's dilated eyes swiveled. "You're not thinkin' of going back there? Not after you've seen them?"

"I am."

"You're crazy, mister! They'll do to us what they did to Sedge! I ain't going." Forgetting himself, Arlo cried shrilly. "You hear me? I ain't!"

"Hush, dang it!" Flavius said, clamping a hand over the man's mouth. "They can hear you in New Orleans!" He swung toward the clearing, afraid the warriors would return. Butterflies flitted wildly in his stomach as minutes crawled by. When he felt it was safe, he seized Kastner and dragged him from the thicket, saying, "On your feet. You're coming whether you like it or not."

"Please!" Arlo begged. "Tie me up. Leave me here. Anything—just don't make me go with you."

"Tell me what happened."

The river rat sat up and clasped his knees. He coughed twice, clenched his fists until the knuckles were white, and said, "They attacked at first light. Had us surrounded. Must have snuck up during the night." Arlo coughed again. "I was on guard from midnight till dawn, and I guess I dozed off. First I knew, one of the darkies hollered. I jumped up, but those Injuns were already in camp. Some of 'em grabbed me while others took my guns."

"They know what guns are then?"

Arlo's pursed his lips. "I reckon they must. Anyhow, the darkies were all whoopin' and tryin' to run, but they couldn't go anywhere chained like they were. One of the women was screamin' like a banshee. That was when Sedge cut loose. He shot one of the hairy devils. Those holdin' me let me go to go after him, and I ran."

"You're not so brave when you don't have the upper hand."

"Go to Hell!" Kastner jabbed a finger upward. "I'd like to have seen you do any different."

"Go on."

The river rat blanched. "I was almost to the trees, and I looked back just as Sedge shot another one. Then seven of them were on him, tearin' the rifle from his hands, and his hand from his arm."

"What?"

"Honest to God. One of those things tore Sedge's right hand from his arm. Another tore off the arm itself. Then—" Arlo gagged, recovered, and finished. "Then a third one took hold of Sedge's throat and ripped the throat right out. I stopped, I was so stunned. And I saw that same Injun take a bite of Sedge's throat and chew it like it was jerky."

Flavius felt his knees go weak. "They ate him? Right then and there?"

"Started to. Another was suckin' on Sedge's wrist when I lit a shuck." Arlo began trembling again. "Do you savvy now, bumpkin? If we go back, those bastards might catch us. And I, for one, don't relish the notion of ending my days in a stew pot."

Neither did Flavius. They were courting a grisly death. And for what? To try and save twenty blacks whom they didn't owe a thing?

No, that wasn't quite right. Twenty *people*. Skin color didn't matter. The blacks were human beings, and humans owed it to one another to help out when someone was in need.

What was it his wife was always quoting? "Do unto others as you would have them do unto you." A grand idea, but awful hard to live by. Especially at moments like this.

"So what's it going to be?" Arlo demanded. "Do we head for the coast? Or for New Orleans? Texas is too far."

Flavius shook his head.

"You can't mean . . . ?"

The Tennessean seized the river rat by the wrist and hauled him toward the clearing. "You can walk. Or I can truss you up and carry you. Which will it be?"

"May you rot in Hell!" Arlo rasped, rising. "We're dead. Do you hear me? Dead!"

"Lead the way." Flavius shoved him, then followed. It didn't help any that deep down inside, he agreed.

Chapter Eight

The best hunters were always the best trackers. That was what the hill folk of Tennessee believed, and rightly so.

A backwoodsman worthy of the name must be expert at the craft. And craft it was. It took diligent effort, over a span of years, to become proficient.

A man must memorize all the different kinds of tracks and be able to tell one creature's from another's. A wolf's from a coyote's. A robin's from a jay's. A salamander's from a lizard's.

A truly competent tracker could determine an animal's size and weight, and thus the approximate age. Sometimes, in conjunction with other factors, even the sex. A good tracker could gauge the creature's weight. Would know whether it had been running or walking or hopping. And so much more.

In short, a skilled tracker could read any creature like a proverbial book just from a few prints.

Davy Crockett was rated one of the best by his kinsmen and friends, and he had earned their esteem honestly. All those years he had spent in the woods as a youngster had paid off. All those hours devoted to learning all he could about all kinds of tracks. To understanding how everything that might effect a print did.

The things he had done to hone his skill! Like those times he'd sat out in the rain to see how the rainfall eroded sign. Or the time when he'd camped next to bear prints for three days to note typical changes. Wind, rain, snow, frost, he knew what all of them did. He had even dug select tracks out of soft soil and taken them home just so he could observe them over long periods.

When anyone needed a bear tracked down, they called on Davy. When someone was being harassed by a predator, they paid the Crockett cabin a visit. When the army needed reliable scouts during the Creek War, one of the men they relied on most was Davy Crockett.

He was never more grateful for his ability than now. It had taken almost half the previous morning, wasting precious hours, but he had finally found the slavers' trail and pursued them for the rest of the day.

Night caught him in the open, his quest unfulfilled. Heeding Bowie's advice, he'd made a small fire on a knoll, building a lean-to to screen it from potentially unfriendly eyes. He'd attempted to sleep, but it was futile. Tossing and turning, he could think of nothing but catching up to Flavius.

The next morning brought surprise after surprise. He found where his friend had spent the night in a tree. At its base were the deeply imbedded manlike footprints of a creature with only *three toes*. There were other bizarre tracks, those of a gigantic beast impossible to identify. And close by were the prints of nine Indians.

But what Indians! The warriors were barefoot! In the swamp! The soles of their feet were heavily callused, their toes bigger than average. Whoever they were, they appeared to be after the slavers.

Davy saw where Flavius had climbed down and continued on. It disturbed him immensely. The safe thing to do was to turn around, to get out of there.

The tracks told him his friend had later met up with one of the river rats. Arlo Kastner, judging by the excessively worn left heel. Davy noted where the pair had ducked into a thicket, and figured out the reason.

Davy put two and two together. Arlo had been running, fleeing, when he stumbled on Flavius. Apparently, the Indians had attacked the slavers, and only Kastner had gotten away.

It was not terribly difficult to guess why Flavius had gone on. The slaves. His friend wanted to save the blacks. A worthy ambition, but it might get Flavius killed.

Davy jogged faster, holding to a dogtrot that ate up the miles. He paralleled their tracks, practically reading his friend's state of mind at each stage.

Flavius and Arlo had gone slowly at first, taking short, measured steps, scared but game. Or at least Flavius was. Arlo had repeatedly dug in his heels, evidently trying to persuade Flavius to turn back before it was too late. Flavius had refused.

They had slowed even more when they neared the camp. Davy saw it himself, off through the trees in a large clearing.

Buzzards were clustered in the center. Their presence assured Davy no Indians were in the area. He strode boldly on out, then stopped cold, his gut seething. To the left lay a human leg. A black leg, a man's, a shackle still on the ankle. Frayed strips of flesh hinted it had been forcibly ripped from the man's body. The body itself was missing. Pools of blood marked two spots where someone had fallen. Smaller scarlet puddles were scattered at random.

Davy walked toward the buzzards, who eyed him warily. "Shoo!" he said, waving his arms. "Scat!" They did, rising into the sky on ponderous wings and circling, waiting for him to leave.

The remains they had been feasting on were those of a white man. It had to be Sedge, yet there was not enough of him left to prove it. Shredded buckskin hung in tatters on exposed rib bones. One of the hands was missing, while the fingers on the other had been pecked clean of flesh down to the bone. The same with the face. The legs were fairly intact, although the vultures had eaten away at the inner thighs.

Tracks led off to the north, deeper into the swamp.

Flavius and the river rat had followed. Davy's best guess was that they had a two-hour lead, give or take thirty minutes. The day was still young, so catching up to them before sunset should not pose a problem. Producing his tomahawk, he blazed a tree at the camp's edge. For Bowie's sake.

Davy took pemmican from his bag and munched as he ran. He'd not eaten a decent meal in days, and he only drank when he was extremely thirsty. As a result, he was half-starved, tired, and sore. But he was not about to give up until Flavius was safe—or those who harmed him had received their just deserts.

Flavius and Arlo were moving faster. Probably because the barefoot Indians were covering ground at twice the speed most men could.

Bogs became more common, and had to be carefully skirted. Twice Davy came on brackish pools that gave off a sulfurous stench. The vegetation was thicker, virtually impassable in certain areas. Gloom pervaded the swamp like a shroud.

Every hundred yards, Davy blazed another tree. Or, when there were no trees, he slashed at the brush, creating crude arrows that pointed in the right direction.

Davy was making excellent time when he noticed gray clouds to the west. Soon the breeze grew gusty and laden with the scent of moisture. Davy hurried, afraid the storm would strike and obliterate the trail. He was in such a hurry that he made a grave mistake. He neglected to keep his eyes on the terrain ahead.

Beyond some pools grew a stand of trees. Davy was so intent on the tracks that he did not look up as he entered. So it was that he *sensed* he was no longer alone before he saw anyone. Halting, he dropped into a crouch, but he was too late.

There were two of them. Gaunt, hairy specimens, lurking in shadows. Motionless figures who stared at him from under beetling brows with eyes as dull as blank slate. Whether they were stragglers from the war party was irrelevant.

Trying to make the best of a bad blunder, Davy stood up and plastered a smile on his face. "Pleased to make your acquaintance," he said. "I don't mean you any harm." He leaned Liz against his side and resorted to the sign talk taught him by the Sioux, holding his hands out so the pair could see his fingers.

They watched, glassy-eyed. Dim-witted brutes, Davy reasoned. Incapable of learning much of anything, let alone complicated sign language. He tried again, saying aloud, "I'm hunting for a friend of mine. I don't want trouble."

The warriors looked at one another. Davy entertained the hope that maybe, just maybe, they gleaned he was friendly and would help. Reality dashed his hope to smithereens when both raised large war clubs, howled like wolves on a hot scent, and sprang.

Davy snatched Liz and backed up. He did not want to shoot if he could help it. The blast might be heard by the war party. He pointed Liz at the man on the right, thinking the threat would be enough to deter them. He should have known better. They separated, one coming at him from the right, one from the left. The former was inches from Liz's muzzle when Davy stroked the trigger.

One down. But the other was on Davy in a twinkling. The club smashed against Liz and sent her sailing. Davy instantly dropped his hands to his flintlocks, but the warrior let go of the war club and flung both arms wide, enfolding Davy in a bear hug.

Throwing himself backward, the Tennessean strained but could not break free. They collided with a tree, careened off, and smacked against another.

The man's brutish features were contorted in bestial fury. He drove a knee up and in, and would have connected with Davy's groin had Davy not twisted, causing them to totter. They bounced off yet another trunk, then staggered out of the stand toward a pool. Davy heaved and bucked and pushed, but it was like attempting to pry steel bars apart.

The warrior's leg and his locked, and they fell.

Davy landed on the bottom in high grass. The Indian applied more pressure, his face red from his exertion. Pain lanced Davy's arms, and he could feel his rib cage begin to buckle. The hairy warrior was tremendously strong, the strongest man Davy had ever gone up against. He wrenched to the left, his shoulders rippling. It had no effect. The hairy brute was slowly but surely squeezing the life from him.

Then the warrior did something even more horrifying. He grinned, exposing his front teeth. *They had been filed to sharp points!*

Davy could not comprehend why anyone would want to mutilate their teeth so horribly. As if in answer, the man's head dipped and those pointy teeth sank into his shoulder, biting through the buckskin and into his flesh. Blood spurted.

The pain was as nothing compared to the shock. Davy felt the man's teeth work back and forth. *The brute was gnawing on him!*

Revulsion spurred Davy into pumping up off the ground, using his hips and feet. He rolled to the left, but did not succeed in dislodging his attacker. The man's teeth grated deeper, and it was all Davy could do not to scream.

Taking a cue from the warrior, Davy rammed his own knee up. A gurgling growl was proof he had scored where it hurt the most. He did it again, and again. After the fourth blow, the man's grip weakened just enough for Davy to break loose.

Davy immediately pushed upright. His hairy antagonist was much slower, giving Davy time to palm his tomahawk. He braced his legs, prepared for whatever the man would try next. Or so he thought.

Roaring like a grizzly, the Indian lowered his head and charged. He slammed into the Tennessean's stomach, his momentum bearing them both backward—into the pool.

Water closed around Davy as he swung. The tomahawk landed, but not solidly. He was forced under, and felt the water pour into his nostrils and ears. He swung a second time, but it was deflected. Iron fingers closed on his neck. Thick thumbs gouged into his windpipe. The Indian sought to drown or strangle him, whichever came first.

Davy could see the man's feral features, just above the surface. He sliced the tomahawk in a half circle, and saw the edge sink in, behind the ear. Scarlet sprayed everywhere. The warrior lurched back, clutching at his head.

Propelling himself erect, Davy greedily gulped fresh breaths. The Indian turned and headed for land, for the war club. Davy lurched after him, but the man reached the weapon and spun. They both stood still, taking each other's measure.

The hairy brute paid no regard to the gash or the blood. Circling, he cocked his powerful arm.

Davy stepped in the opposite direction, staying just out of reach. He sought to trick his foe into lunging, into over-extending himself. But the warrior was more clever than Davy gave him credit for; he didn't take the bait.

The Tennessean moved toward shore, only to be thwarted when the Indian sidestepped to bar his path. Davy went further, but the man did the same. Strangely enough, the warrior seemed intent on keeping him in the pool.

Davy was baffled. What could his enemy hope to accomplish? A little water never hurt anybody. *True,* a voice in his skull agreed, *but what was* in *the water could*. He whirled. Several yards out and closing fast was an alligator. Rather puny as gators went, it measured maybe six feet from snout to tail. But there was nothing puny about its glistening teeth. It surged in close, mouth agape.

Mentally cursing himself for not having enough brains to grease a skillet, Davy leaped toward dry ground. But the warrior was waiting. Davy was caught between a rock and a hard place. Or in this case, between razor-rimmed jaws and a heavy war club.

"Damn."

There was once chance, slim as it might be. Davy took another bound toward shore anyway, the gator at his very heels. Predictably, the warrior came to meet him. At the last instant, Davy darted to the right.

Now the reptilian beast and the man-brute were face-to-face. The alligator attacked, seeking to bite the Indian's leg. An agile spring carried the man to safety. Then, turning, the warrior swept the war club down on top of the gator's head.

Davy scurried out of the pool. He thought the warrior had temporarily forgotten about him, but the man drove at him in a savage whirlwind. Davy warded off several swings, retreating to the right as he did.

Inexplicably, the Indian stopped and grinned.

Now what? Davy wondered. And received his answer when a clammy sensation spread up over his moccasins. *How could that be when he was a good five feet from the water's edge?* He risked a glance down, and his heart skipped a beat.

It wasn't water.

It was quicksand.

"I'm not takin' another step."

Flavius Harris halted and turned. The river rat had folded his arms and planted his legs. "Is that so?" Flavius said.

"Yep, it is," Arlo Kastner declared. "Go ahead. Shoot me

if you want. But I don't reckon you will. Not when those stinkin' ghouls are so close.''

Flavius was sorely tempted. All Arlo did was gripe, gripe, gripe. Griped worse than Matilda, and *that* took some doing. But the cutthroat had a point. They had almost caught up with the slaves and their inhuman captors. A shot was bound to give them away.

''So let's part company with no hard feelin's, eh?'' Arlo proposed. ''Give me a pistol and your knife and I'll be on my way.''

''No.''

The river rat gestured angrily. ''I've put up with as much of your nonsense as I aim to. If you have a hankerin' to get yourself killed, go right ahead. I sure as hell won't stop you. All I want is a chance to protect myself.''

''Forget it.''

Mad as a blind hornet, Arlo took a step and shook a fist under the Tennessean's nose. ''Listen to me, bumpkin. We've been plumb lucky so far. But no one's luck holds forever. And in case you ain't noticed, all the signs points to us being mighty near a village. This whole area is probably crawlin' with hairy demons.''

Flavius *had* noticed. But it did not deter him from his purpose. He would save the blacks or he would die trying. As Davy was so fond of saying, it was root hog or die.

''Come on,'' Arlo said. ''Let me have a pistol. Just one. I'll be out of your hair and you can go get eaten.'' His eyes narrowed. ''I don't rightly see what you're tryin' to prove anyway. Those darkies don't mean anything to you or me. So why go to all this bother? Why get yourself killed on their miserable account?''

''You'd never understand.''

''Why? Are you sayin' you're smarter than me? Or are you one of those Bible-bangers? You doing this because it's the Christian thing to do?''

How could Flavius explain? His motive was too deeply personal. He owed it to the blacks, yes, but he also owed it to himself. He had something to prove, something important. "Right is right," he simply answered.

"What in hell does that mean?" Arlo snickered. "Stupid is stupid too. Which is why I ain't going any further. Hand over a gun."

Flavius had tried to reason. But he wasn't a talker, like Davy. He didn't have a flair for flowery words or a talent for persuading others. And when all else failed, the best approach to a problem was always the direct approach. Giving no inkling of his intent, he started to turn away.

"Hold on," Arlo said, and reached for him.

Flavius rammed Matilda's muzzle into the riverrat's abdomen. Hard. Kastner folded like a fan, onto his knees, and retched. Flavius waited for the spasm to subside, then said quietly, "You'll do as I say, not the other way around. What you want to do counts for a hill of beans, far as I'm concerned. And whether the Indians kill you or I do, it's all the same to me."

Arlo looked up, ablaze with raw hatred. "If it's the last thing I ever do—!" he wheezed, stopping when Flavius raised the rifle.

"And another thing," Flavius said. "No more threats. My friend told me once that it's what we *do,* not what we *say* we'll do, that counts."

"Shoot me, then. 'Cause this is as far as I go."

"Think again." Flavius was not going to bandy words. They had no more time to squander. He kicked the river rat in the side, and when Kastner was rolling in agony, he kicked him again. As he lifted his foot to stomp on him, the ruffian frantically thrust an open palm at him and bleated like a goat.

"Enough! Damn you! Enough!"

"On your feet."

If a glare could kill, Flavius would have been shriveled by

the one Arlo bestowed on him. Putting on a show of being in great anguish, the cutthroat rose, his arms crisscrossed over his midsection. "I just hope they eat you first. Raw. I want to see the look on your face when they take their first bite."

Flavius motioned. "After you."

Gnarled trees cloaked in vines reared above them. Undergrowth choked with leaves and limbs limited how far they could see in any given direction to a dozen feet at most. The ground was soft, even by the swamp's standards, dirt clinging to their feet at every step.

Flavius felt uneasy. It was a place fit for neither man nor beast, and the animals apparently agreed, because he had not heard a bird chirp or squirrel chitter or any other creature for quite some time. Normally it meant a predator was abroad, but Flavius had not seen a trace of one. Or much else. Animal tracks had been abundant; now they were few and far between. It was almost as if the wildlife had fled. Or been wiped out.

Arlo grew as jumpy as a long-tailed cat in a room full of rocking chairs. Constantly scouring the vegetation, he skulked along on the tips of his toes, poised for flight at the slightest threat. "I don't like this, bumpkin," he whispered.

Flavius didn't either. A feeling came over him that unseen eyes were upon them. He blamed it on bad nerves, but he was fooling no one, especially himself. When a shadow deep in the brush moved, his worst fear was made real. "They're on to us," he announced.

The river rat drew up short. "What? You're sure?" Panic radiated from him like light from the sun. "Then let's skedaddle, while we have the use of our legs!"

"It wouldn't do any good."

"How can you be sure?"

"They're all around us."

Pure speculation, but Flavius had a hunch he was right. The problem now was how to save the blacks and get out of cannibal country with their hides and hair intact. "Act casual. Don't let on you're afraid."

"That should be easy, since I'm *not*." Arlo hooked his thumbs in his pants and whistled as if he did not have a care in the world. His choice of songs was a bawdy tune popular in taverns and saloons called "Jenny's Scandal."

Flavius knew it well. It had to do with a young woman who sews herself a dress sporting a hem two inches above her ankles. The community is outraged, and some biddies pay her a visit to demand she conform to rules of common decency. So Jenny raises the hem another two inches.

"My God!" Arlo suddenly exclaimed. "Look behind us!"

A hairy man-brute was right out in the open, smack in the middle of the trail, spiked war club at his side, silently staring.

Flavius kept on walking, and advised his reluctant companion to do the same. They were doomed—as good as dead—yet, oddly, he experienced little fear. The riverrat, on the other hand, showed the true hue of his backbone.

Arlo commenced shaking like an aspen leaf, and his teeth set to chattering like a chipmunk's. "I don't want to die," he whimpered. "We should make a break for it now. You go west, I'll go east. And the Devil take the hindmost." He started to sidle toward the brush.

Flavius snagged his arm. "Don't even think it. You wouldn't get twenty feet."

"How the hell do you know?" Arlo grated, tugging.

"I have eyes," Flavius responded, and nodded at the woods.

One moment they weren't there, the next they were. A score or more of tousle-haired warriors had materialized out of nowhere, on both sides. As grimly still as a row of tombstones, they merely stared.

"Noooooo!" the river rat groaned. He turned to run off, but Flavius would not release him. "Please! Before it's too late!"

"It already is."

The trail broadened, ending at a wide field. Structures were visible. People were moving about.

"Lordy!" Arlo breathed. "It's their village!"

No one tried to stop them from entering, but Flavius suspected it would be a different story should they seek to leave. He halted at sight of the slaves in a crude rickety pen beside a long low lodge constructed mainly of brush and limbs.

The rest of the lodges were small conical affairs, each with a single low door but no windows. Women dressed in short animal-hide skirts were busy at various tasks. Some sewed, some scraped hides, some chopped roots or kneaded an unusual reddish dough, while others tended to infants. Older children scampered playfully about, as children everywhere would do. Warriors, for the most part, were huddled in groups, talking or sharpening the spikes on their war clubs.

Suddenly, a gray-haired man screeched like a panther. All activity ceased. All eyes swung toward the Tennessean and the river rat.

Flavius glanced over a shoulder. Escape was out of the question. More warriors were filing from the woods and fanning out.

"I knew it! I just knew it!" Arlo lamented, turning right and left like a coon at bay. "I should have made you shoot me!" He edged toward the tree line. "You can stay if you want, damn your bones. But not me! I'm leaving, and there's—" His gaze drifted to the long lodge, and a hand shot to his mouth.

In the shade of an overhang was a huge pot made entirely of clay. Large enough to hold two or three sizeable gators, Flavius observed. Only the inhabitants seem to prefer different fare. Ghastly fare.

"Kill me now!" Arlo said.

Jutting over the rim of the pot, bent at the elbow, was the partially devoured remains of a human arm.

Chapter Nine

Quicksand! The mere word was enough to spawn terror. Of all the secret fears woodsmen harbored, being caught in quicksand was near the top of the list. No one should have to suffer such a lingering, horrid death.

Sentiments Davy Crockett categorically agreed with. Ordinarily, he gave quicksand and bogs wide berths.

He still remembered that day during his eighth year when a neighbor's ox had blundered into a nearby marsh. The animal had been up to its belly in quicksand when it was found. Word spread rapidly, and men came to help from miles around. They tried everything. They threw ropes, they used long poles, they stretched a log across to lever the ox out, but all their efforts were for naught.

Davy had been on the bank with the women and a dozen or so children. It had been highly entertaining at first, a break in the daily routine, an excuse to get out of doing chores.

When the ox sank in up to its neck, it had fully dawned on Davy that the animal might die. He'd hollered encouragement to the frantic men, just as the rest were doing, but all the shouting and yelling in the world could not stave off the outcome.

At the very end, the ox bellowed. A pitiable cry, a peal of misery, it sent a shiver down Davy's young spine. He saw men strain on ropes that had been thrown over the animal's head, saw others attempt to worm poles under the animal. Methods that had not worked before did not work then.

Like a rock sinking slowly into soft mud, the ox sank from sight, the quicksand flowing up over its horns, its ears, its wide eyes. To the last, it tried to go on breathing. Bubbles frothed the surface, and there was a mighty upheaval, then all was still.

Some of the women and children cried. The men hung their heads. Davy had been sad for days. He'd petted that ox a few times, fed it corn and such.

The lesson he learned had been invaluable. When the life of an animal as big and strong as an ox could be snuffed out so easily, so could his. He'd been very cautious in the wilderness from that day forth.

But a fat lot of good his caution had done him now! Davy saw quicksand ooze up around his ankles, and he did what anyone would do. He lunged toward solid ground. Unfortunately, the brute-man anticipated him, and pounced, swinging the war club at him. Davy had to back away or be bashed.

The quicksand was up above his ankles. Movement made him sink faster. Yet if he didn't move, if he didn't get out of there quickly, he would share the ox's fate.

His pistols had been soaked when he fell into the pool, but he drew the left one anyway, cocked it, and took aim. The hairy warrior showed no fear, standing there as brazen as brass. Davy prayed for the best and pulled the trigger.

The flintlock misfired.

Shoving it under his belt, Davy drew the other one. The quicksand had gained another couple of inches, but he could still move his legs. He angled to the right, the warrior staying with him. Centering a bead on the man's forehead, Davy fired. A puff of smoke, a flash of flame—and nothing else. The powder had been too damp. Replacing it at his waist, he resorted to a desperate gambit.

Davy had developed a fondness for the tomahawk. Many settlers looked down their noses at the weapon, saying it could not begin to rival a trusty butcher knife. The edge was shorter, it was harder to throw; a "silly savage's weapon," they branded it.

Davy knew better. A tomahawk was as versatile as it was deadly. The Creeks had proven that during the war. Properly used, it could hold its own against any knife, ax, or sword. On a stump out behind his cabin he'd painted a white circle, and for hours on end, day after day, he'd practiced with his, growing more and more skilled, until he could embed it in the circle ten times out of ten.

It was a talent that often came in handy. Such as now.

Davy drew his knife with his left hand. He made a show of preparing to throw it, and did so, knowing full well he lacked the power in his left arm that he had in his right, and that the warrior would avoid it with no problem.

Which the brute did. The knife landed in grass, and the Indian looked at it and grinned. He should have kept his eyes on Davy.

The tomahawk streaked back, flashed forward. Handle and head swirled end over end. Hearing the *swish,* the Indian glanced up. The edge sheared into the bridge of his nose, parting the flesh as neatly as a dagger would, penetrating deep. For several seconds he was motionless, blood and gore flowing freely. Then he took a halting step toward the quicksand, lifted his heavy club, and died.

Davy had disposed of one problem, but he still had another. The quicksand was almost to his knees. He moved, or tried to; his legs would barely budge. The quicksand clung to him like liquid lead. And the attempt made him sink faster. Desperate, he surged maybe half a foot, and lost four more inches of leg.

Trying not to think of the consequences of failure, Davy girded himself for another effort. This time he used his head. He eased his legs forward one at a time, by gradual degrees. It seemed to work. He was eighteen or nineteen inches from solid ground. Then fifteen. Twelve. He extended an arm toward a bush, to grab it for added leverage.

Suddenly, disaster. The quicksand shot up as high as his chest. Davy froze. He stopped sinking for the moment, but it was small consolation. The bush was well out of reach. The solid ground might as well have been on the moon.

Davy tried to recall all the advice he had been given. "Lie on your back and you'll float," one man had claimed, "then you can wriggle to shore." Another veteran of the wilds had suggested that he "lay on your side and roll real quick-like. Half the time it works real well." The fellow had not mentioned what happened the other half of the time.

Davy craned his neck, searching for a means of saving his life. Other than the bush, nothing else was close enough. And the bush itself was puny, perhaps too puny to support his weight.

"I reckon I'm in pretty considerable of a bind," Davy said, just to hear his own voice.

Someone answered. Or, rather, *something* did. The alligator grunted and swiveled. Davy had forgotten about it. He'd assumed it was dead, that the warrior's club had crushed its brainpan. Although bleeding profusely, however, it was very much alive. And its maw, filled with sawtooth death, was opening and closing as if the reptile were eager to feast on him.

"Never give up!" his grandma had often told him. "Where there's life, there's hope," was another of her sayings. Yet at that moment, Davy Crockett's wellspring of hope dwindled drastically as the gator slunk nearer. He saw no way out. If the quicksand didn't claim him, the alligator would. Or maybe when the gator attacked, *both* of them would be borne under.

The beast moved with exaggerated slowness. Perhaps the head wound was to blame. Or maybe it was not quite sure where he was since he was not moving and gators relied on movement to pinpoint prey.

Davy watched it slink to within a few feet of the quicksand, then halt. It seemed to be staring right at him, yet it did not do anything except blink. Davy did not even do that, for fear the animal would strike.

The alligator looked to either side. Grunting, it lifted its right foreleg while bending to the right, and veered toward the water. It was not going to eat him, after all. Its long tail curved in an S in its wake.

The tail! Davy extended his other arm as the tail slowly slid toward him. What he proposed to do was insane, but it was his only hope. The tail whipped left, whipped right, whipped left again. Then the thing was right in front of him, and Davy grabbed hold and clung on with all his might.

The alligator lashed around, hissing like a snake, but could not quite reach him. In a flurry, it hurtled toward the pool and sanctuary, its short legs pumping. For its size, it was a mass of muscle. Much stronger than the Tennessean. But was it strong enough?

The tail's serrated crest was as rough to the touch as a dry hide, the scales as slippery as glass. Davy dug in his nails, his muscles corded into compact bands. His body gave a lurch and started to slide upward, but the quicksand was not to be denied. It wrapped around him like a two-ton glove, holding fast.

A tug of war ensued. The gator against the quagmire. The reptile was as straight as an arrow, claws scraping as it heaved forward.

Davy sought to help by kicking with both legs. A sucking

noise granted the illusion the quicksand was losing its grip, but just when his body began to move, he was brought to a stop. The next couple of minutes were ordeals in themselves. The gator churned and churned. Presently, it would tire, and that would be that.

No! Davy fumed. Where there was a will, there was a way! If the alligator couldn't do it on its own, he would give it added incentive. He punched the tail. Once, twice, three times. He was drawing his arm back for a fourth blow when the creature grunted and scrambled forward with newfound energy.

The sucking noise was repeated, louder than before. It felt as if a hundred tiny hands were pulling at Davy. Then, abruptly, he was yanked bodily up out of the muck and was swung to the left. Releasing his unwilling helper, he rolled a few times, coming to rest on his side facing the pool. The gator was in the water, diving from sight.

"I'm obliged, ugly," Davy said.

Weariness nipped at him, but he shrugged it off. He would rest when Flavius was safe. About to sit up, he tensed when a shadow fell across his chest. *Another warrior,* he guessed, and cast about for the knife he had thrown.

"Partial to mud baths, are you? I hear tell the well-to-do in Europe spend hundreds of dollars to have themselves plastered with the stuff. Which goes to show you just how dumb people can be."

Davy squinted up at the tall frontiersman. "Took your sweet time catching up. Stop to smell the flowers, did you?"

"Hell, I came quick as I could," James Bowie said. "I had to leave Sam. He was groggy yet. Might have a mild concussion. So I built him a lean-to, gave him a rifle and a pistol, and got here in time to see that scaly friend of yours pulling you out." Bowie grinned. "You do things like this often?"

Making a comment about Bowie's ancestry, Davy sat up.

Bowie chuckled and began to gather the Tennessean's weapons. "If I hadn't seen it with my own eyes, I'd never believe it. Funny thing is, no one I tell will believe it either. Even tall tales have their limits."

Davy did not see the humor in the situation. "We're not far behind Flavius and Kastner." Rising, he brushed at the quicksand that clung to his buckskins, but it was too thick and gooey to remove by hand. He went to the pool, set his pistols down, and warily waded in. The alligator did not show itself as he ducked under up to his shoulders and hastily cleaned himself off.

Bowie was examining the two flintlocks. "It would take forever to clean these."

"Then they'll have to wait." Davy accepted them, dunked each once, and tucked them where they belonged. He reloaded his rifle, cleaned off his tomahawk and knife, and was ready.

They took up the chase with sober intensity. The Tennessean led. Although he was tired and hurting, he did not slack off. Intuition warned him he must find Flavius soon. *Very* soon.

Davy hoped his friend was well, and wondered what Flavius was doing at that exact moment.

Had the Irishman only known, he would have begged the powers that be for the fleetness of fabled Mercury.

For at that very second Flavius Harris was bound hand and foot, his arms behind his back, lying in a small conical lodge. The interior was as murky as a coal cellar. He could barely distinguish the outline of Arlo Kastner.

"You're a jackass," the river rat complained for the umpteenth time. "You should have shot a couple. The rest would have backed off and we could have escaped. Now look. Slated for the cookin' pot, thanks to you."

"If I'd killed one, we'd be dead," Flavius said. He had

123

brought Matilda to bear when the hairy warriors converged. He had even fixed his sights on the gray-haired man, who appeared to be their leader, but he couldn't bring himself to shoot. The Indians had stripped him of his weapons, trussed the two of them like hogs fit for slaughter, and thrown them into the lodge.

That had been hours ago. The afternoon was waning. Soon it would be time for the evening meal, and Flavius shuddered to think what—or rather, *who*—the main course would be.

"I should have made sure you were dead when I fed you to the gators," Arlo groused. "You're the reason I'm in this mess, fat man."

"Don't blame me. Blame your greed."

Arlo swore, and hiked himself into a seated position. "Don't act so high-and-mighty. You'd do the same if you thought you could get away with it." He leaned against the wall, dry brush crackling. "A fella can't be blamed for tryin' to get ahead in this world. It's every man for himself, in case you ain't heard."

"I don't believe that, and I never will," Flavius said. "Most folks are naturally good, not evil. Take my partner, Crockett. Know what his family motto is?"

"I don't care."

"Always be sure you're right, then go ahead," Flavius quoted. "He learned it from his pa, who learned it from *his* pa. And so on. Law-abiding, decent people who would give you the shirt off their backs if you were that much in need." He sat up too. "So much for everyone being as crooked as a dog's hind leg. The Crockett clan proves most people have hearts of gold."

"The only thing they prove," Arlo said, "is that being dumb runs in their family."

Flavius had a retort on the tip of his tongue, but the deer hide covering the door parted and in came the gray-haired man. The top elder, as it were. "Howdy," Flavius said, smiling. "We sure would like to palaver a spell, to show you we're friendly."

Kastner fluttered his lips, then said, "You're pathetic, bumpkin. I'm surprised you didn't strangle yourself with your own diaper when you were little."

The elder looked from one to the other. Bending, he ran his hands over Flavius's shoulders, ribs, and stomach, and pinched Flavius above the hips.

"What in tarnation is that coyote doing?" Arlo asked. "Ticklin' you?"

"Not hardly." Flavius had done the same many times, to pigs and sheep and cows he'd had to slaughter. The oldster was gauging how much meat he had on his bones.

Arlo recoiled when it was his turn. "Take your rotten hands off me!" he bellowed. Elevating his boots, he drove them at the Indian's face, but the man swatted them aside with deceptive ease for one so advanced in years. Arlo was knocked off balance, landing on his back. The elder calmly straddled him and repeated what he had done to Flavius.

"If it's the last think I ever do, you mangy Injun, I'm going to kill you!"

"Don't make it any worse than it already is," Flavius said.

Brittle mirth cascaded from the river rat. "What a moron! I'm going to die alongside an idiot. And there's nothin' I can do about it."

After completing his examination, the elder left. The flap swung down, but not quite all the way. Sparkling sunlight streamed in through the gap.

Flavius scooted his backside over. Peeking out, he saw the oldster talking to another man. Others were carting deadwood from the swamp and piling it around the huge clay pot. The village bustled with activity. It did not take a genius to realize the Indians were preparing for a special celebration.

Arlo had sat back up. Wagging his wrists, he said, "Chew on my ropes. When I'm free, I'll untie you."

Two warriors strode around the corner of the long lodge, ushering a young black woman between them. Her arms were bound, but the leg irons were gone.

"Who had the keys to the shackles?" Flavius inquired.

"Huh? What does that matter?"

"Who?"

"Sedge did. He didn't trust me to keep 'em because I was always losin' the damn things. Which was fine by me. The ring they were on must have weighed five pounds."

The black woman was taken before the elder. He gave her the same treatment he had given Flavius and the river rat. She held her head high, but her full lips quivered. At a word from the chief, she was guided into the long lodge instead of being returned to the holding pen.

Flavius leaned his brow against a bent sapling that formed part of the frame, and closed his eyes. *That poor woman.* He had never felt so helpless. Or so guilty. For the simple truth was that the Africans would not be in danger if more people did as the Quakers were doing and spoke out against slavery.

But his guilt ran deeper than that. For once in his life he had tried to make a difference, tried to do what was right. He had stood on his own two feet. He had risked everything to help those in need. And he had failed. Failed miserably. Now the blacks would pay for his failure with their lives.

"Come on, damn it," Arlo said. "Get me loose."

Flavius roused himself. "How big a fool do you think I am?" he responded. "Free me first, then I'll do the same for you."

"You don't trust me?"

"No," Flavius bluntly admitted. The cutthroat had to be kidding. Arlo had tried to kill him once already. Flavius slid closer, wrists held out. "What will it be?"

Grumbling, Arlo lowered his mouth to the rope and gnawed like a beaver. The tough strands of hide resisted, and every so often he lifted his head to mutter swear words.

126

Flavius tilted sideways to see outside. The people were retiring to their lodges to prepare for the evening's festivities. The same two warriors who had escorted the black woman from the pen now stood guard in front of the long lodge. As Flavius looked on, several Indian women carrying baskets and bowls hurried into it.

Spittle dribbled onto Flavius's wrists. Arlo was chewing with a vengeance. It would take a while to gnaw clean through, and time was a luxury they did not have much of.

Flavius worried about Davy. The Irishman should have shown up long ago. He fretted that something horrible had happened. Fretted that he was totally on his own.

"Hold still, bumpkin," the river rat chided.

Quite by accident, Flavius had lowered his arms a trifle. They were growing tired. He looked outside, past the long lodge to where a corner of the pen could be seen. Some of the Africans were pacing, other staring at the lodge. Flavius shared their apprehension. Somehow, the woman must be saved.

Arlo straightened and spat. "There. Give it a try."

Half the strands were bitten through. Flavius thrust his arms outward in an attempt to snap the rest, but they were a lot stronger than they appeared. He tried again, and was rewarded with a strand popping.

Feet tramped, and muted voices approached. Sliding away from the river rat, Flavius lay on his back.

Into the lodge ducked the elder and two stoic warriors. "Did you forget something?" the Tennessean asked, placing his hands close to his buttocks so none of the Indians would notice the gnawed rope.

"They probably want to drag you off to that pot," Arlo said, smirking wickedly. "A nice, plump blob of meat like you must make their mouths water."

But it wasn't Flavius they were after. At a gesture from the chief, the warriors stepped to the riverrat and each grasped an arm. Arlo stiffened in disbelief, then jerked backward. "Get your rotten paws off me, you stinkin' cannibals! If you think you can eat me, you have another think comin'."

The elder left.

The other two hoisted Kastner and toted him to the opening. Arlo kicked and screeched. "Don't take me! Take him! Take the bumpkin!" As one of the warriors pushed the flap aside, the slaver went berserk. He threw himself in all directions, twisting and turning, striving to bite them or butt them with his forehead. "No! No! No! I won't let you! Put me down!"

A blow to the jaw silenced him. Arlo slumped as he was carted out, his eyes locking on the Tennessean's in mute appeal.

Flavius moved to the entrance, nosing the flap aside. The warriors were bearing the river rat to the long lodge. Kastner no longer resisted. He seemed overwhelmed by the development, too stunned to fight, his will sapped. As much as Flavius disliked him and resented what Arlo had done, this was not how the man deserved to meet his end. No one did.

Tucking his knees to his chest, Flavius hunched over and attempted to slide his hands under his backside. But his wrists were still so tightly bound that he could not manage more than halfway.

"Where there's a will, there's a way," he stated, and tried again. And again. And yet again.

The rope chafed his skin. His wrists were on fire. He stretched his arms to their limit, and beyond. About to give up, he felt another strand give. His arms slowly scraped forward, then up and around. *He had done it!* In savage joy he bit into the hide, grating his teeth back and forth.

It took forever. Finally the rope was severed. Undoing the knots and those on his ankles was the work of minutes. Flavius flung the ropes into a corner and peered out.

The sun was half gone. Shadows dappled the village. The

only Indians abroad were the guards at the main lodge.

The dwelling in which Flavius had been placed was one of the nearest to the east of the lodge. To reach the pen he must cross a wide-open space, unless he circled around behind the long structure. As soon as it was dark enough to try, he would.

Settling onto his stomach, Flavius waited impatiently. From some of the lodges laughter rose, from others loud voices. The Indians were in fine fettle.

Recollecting the time he was a captive of the Ojibwas, Flavius poked his head out as far as was prudent and scoured the shadows for mongrels. Dogs would spoil everything. Most tribes kept some. Not as pets, but as guardians to sound a warning in case of a raid, and as beasts of burden to pull heavily laden travois. He saw none, which was highly unusual.

Or maybe not.

Whoever these Indians were, they weren't squeamish about what they ate. It could be that humans weren't their only fare. Maybe they ate anything and everything. It would explain why wildlife was scarce in the area.

Someone was out and about. It was the elder, but what a change! He wore a beaded shirt and pants, and a headdress with enough feathers to fill a wheelbarrow. At the long lodge he paused in front of a niche Flavius had overlooked. From it he removed what Flavius took to be a hollow tube, about a yard long. Putting one end to his lips, the elder blew three loud, low notes.

It was a signal for the rest of the tribe, including women and children, to parade in regal procession across the square. Four abreast, they filed into the long lodge. The last to go in were the guards. Soon light spilled out through the wide doorway, and chanting commenced.

Flavius was through waiting. It was now or never. He would rather have his guns, but he did not know where the

Indians had put them. Slipping out, he padded to the right.
The guttural chorus drowned out what little noise he made.
He was almost to the rear corner of the long lodge when the
unforeseen occurred.

Another guard strode from behind it.

Chapter Ten

Davy Crockett and James Bowie had been on the go for over an hour when Davy's left leg developed a cramp. Against his will he had to slow down. Within a few more paces the discomfort was severe enough to force him to halt. Limping to a log, he sat, explaining why as he did.

"A few minutes won't matter much," Bowie said. "I'm a bit winded anyway." Putting his back to a tree, he hunkered down.

Davy begged to differ. "A few minutes can make all the difference in the world. The difference between life and death."

"True enough, I suppose." Bowie sighed. "This Harris sure is lucky to have a friend like you. Here you are, risking everything to save him. Not many people would do what you're doing."

"You would."

Bowie's eyebrow arched. "Think so? You hardly know me, so what makes you say that?"

Davy was massaging his leg vigorously. "Some men wear their character on their sleeves. Deep down, you have true grit. More than most. You'd go out of your way to help someone in need."

"Por meterte a redentor te ha passado todo esto."

"You speak Spanish too?"

James Bowie nodded. "I can read and write Spanish, French, and English. And I know half-a-dozen Indian tongues. A few black dialects too." He smiled. "I have a gift, my brother claims. He says I should go into politics."

"Funny. My friends say the same about me."

"But I'm not as pure as you make me out to be, friend," Bowie remarked. "At one time or another I've broken nearly all the Commandments. Especially that one about not coveting what your neighbor has." He spoke softly, as if to himself. "God help me, but I covet money more than anything. Wealth. Luxury. I've had a taste of how the very rich live, and I aim to live just like they do some day. Some day soon."

Davy sensed a certain sadness in the man, a certain self-reproach. "And you figure Black Ivory is the means to your end?"

Bowie sighed again. "I'll be frank. Once I did, yes. But the longer I've been at this, the less I like it. So I've tried to fool myself. I tell myself that I'm better than most other slave runners because I treat the blacks better than they do. But the truth is, what I'm doing is wrong."

"Then why not up and end it?"

"The money . . ." Bowie said, his voice trailing off.

"My grandpa used to say that the root of all evil in this world of ours is the love of money."

"Your grandfather was wise."

Trying to cheer Bowie up, Davy commented, "At least you know the value of a dollar. Me, I've never had much interest in being King Midas. I've always been content to go from day to day, taking whatever the Good Lord threw my way."

He laughed lightly. "It about drives my wife crazy. She says I have the least ambition of any man alive. I think she wishes she'd known it when she married me. She'd probably have turned me down."

Bowie smiled. "Women naturally like the finer things in life. And it just so happens that the finer things cost more."

"If you ask me, we'd all be better off if we lived in caves and wore bearskins. Then no one would covet anything."

The tall frontiersman smiled. "You come up with the silliest notions. Has anyone ever told you that?"

"Oh, just about everybody."

Bowie became serious again. "A few more trips, and I think I'll end it. Rezin will have to find another partner or go into another business. I'll be off to the Paris of the West to find my fortune some other way."

"Maybe you should go to Texas," Davy suggested.

"Texas? What's there besides Comanches and run-down old church missions?"

"Oh, you'd be surprised. The people are as friendly as a parson at a fund-raiser. And since you already speak Spanish, you'd be right at home." Davy recalled his long ride from San Antonio. "It's a land of milk and honey, Jim. Beautiful rolling hills and fertile plains. Trees that stretch to the sky. Rivers that never go dry. Sweet grass for horses and cattle. Enough varmints to feed a family for all their days."

"You make it sound like paradise."

"To some it could be. The government is offering land grants, and you could get yourself an estate the size of Rhode Island for pennies. And since I suspect you have a hankering for the ladies, I should let you know that those Mexican gals are as pretty as speckled coon dogs."

"You call that attractive?"

Davy laughed. "To each their own. And to a coon hunter like me, a coon dog is about the prettiest critter in all creation."

"I'll take the ladies any day."

They grinned at one another, both of them seeming to realize they shared a special bond. It was Davy who coughed and stated, "Think about it. You could do worse. If it's wealth you're after, there's plenty to be had there. If land doesn't interest you, you could always search for those lost silver mines."

"Those what?"

"An old-timer in San Antonio told me about them. The San Saba silver mines, they're called. Operated by the Spanish years ago, until the Indians got fed up at being made to do the digging and ran the Spaniards out. Now no one can say exactly where they are. But Indians come into town from time to time with pure silver to trade."

"Silver," Bowie said softly.

"The mines are worth millions. Lots of men have hunted for them, and lots have never been heard from again. But if you're interested, the information is right there in the mission records for you to read."

James Bowie gazed westward. "Texas. It does have a ring, doesn't it?" He shrugged those broad shoulders of his. "Who knows? Maybe I'll pay it a visit one day. Just for the hell of it, you understand."

"Surely."

The cramp was about gone. Standing, Davy tested his leg by walking in a small circle. "Truth is, I might go back there my own self. It really is the garden spot of the world. With the best land prospects I've ever seen." He thought of his chronic mystery ailment. "And a healthy climate, besides."

"All right," Bowie smiled. "I get the idea."

"If you ever do get there, let me know," Davy said. "I'll come join you. Between us we'll own half the territory in no time."

Bowie shook his head in amusement. "You never give up, do you? What do you want, a signed promise I'll go?" Clapping the Tennessean on the shoulder, he moved to the trail. "But first things first. We still have these Indians to deal with."

"Any idea what tribe they are?"

"No. But that's not surprising. There are dozens of small tribes scattered through the swamp. Tribes that keep to themselves, for the most part. Some are supposed to be worse than the Karankawas."

"Speaking of which, do you reckon they're still after us?"

"No telling. It depends on how mad Snake Strangler is. The last time I tangled with him, he chased me over fifty miles."

The Tennessean pumped his leg a few times. "Well, we'd best be on our way."

Bowie started off, then paused and glanced around. "Davy?"

"What?"

"Thank you."

"For what?"

"Just thanks."

With that, James Bowie raced on down the trail, Davy at his heels. Mile after mile was covered in total silence. They were threading through a wooded tract when, unexpectedly, Bowie stopped so suddenly that Davy almost stumbled into him. Bowie raised a finger to his lips, then pointed to the northeast.

A few seconds elapsed before Davy heard them too. Voices. The two men melted into the vegetation, covering a couple of dozen yards before coming on the source.

Three brutish warriors were hiking northward, chattering excitedly. All three carried armloads of deadwood. They were using a well-established trail, a clue their village must be near at hand. Exactly how near was made clear a few minutes later when Davy and James followed them to their dwellings. The trio took the firewood to an enormous clay pot and deposited it around the pot's base.

James Bowie gripped Davy's arm, then pointed.

Davy has seen them too. In a pen beside a long building were the blacks. He did not see any sign of Flavius or Kastner, and he was eager to go back to where the voices had lured James and him off the trail. He whispered his intentions.

"You ago ahead," said Bowie. "I'm staying here."

"Don't do anything foolish while I'm gone."

Retracing their steps, Davy took up where they had left off. He had not gone far when he found where warriors had surprised the pair. That there were no drops of blood or crushed grass was encouraging. The best Davy could tell, Flavius and the river rat had walked on into the village of their own accord.

Where were they now? That was the burning question. Davy hastened to where he had left Bowie, who greeted him with a nod.

"There's been a lot going on. They've been buzzing around like bees in a bonnet. More wood was brought in. One of the African women was taken into that long lodge."

"What about Flavius and Kasnter? They're in there somewhere. The sign proves as much."

"No trace yet." Bowie indicated a gray-haired man talking to two younger warriors. "That old coot seems to give all the orders. He must be their leader." Bowie gazed skyward. "Not much we can do until sundown. Unless you have an idea?"

Davy had to admit he didn't. Sneaking into the village in broad daylight would only earn them a turn in the cook pot. They had to lay low, which was awful hard to do knowing his best friend was a captive of cannibals.

The next few hours were some of the longest of Davy's whole life. Activity stopped when the Indians repaired to their dwellings, leaving a pair of guards in front of the main building and another at the rear. The latter acted bored and leaned against the building, his arms folded.

The sun was ready to relinquish the heavens to stars when a commotion perked up Davy's interest. The chief and two others had just entered a small dwelling. Someone was hollering—*in English*!

The leader reappeared. Moments later so did the other pair, bearing a familiar form.

"Arlo!" Bowie whispered.

The river rat was taken into the longest lodge. Quiet reigned thereafter. Davy did not take his eyes off that small dwelling, and was rewarded when a head poked out. A thrill ran through him. *Flavius was alive!* His friend looked all about, then ducked back inside.

"So far, so good," Bowie said. "But snatching them out of there won't be a cinch."

An understatement, if ever the Irishman heard one. By mutual unspoken agreement they stayed where they were until the shadows congealed into twilight. Davy was rising onto his knees when the chief reappeared, decked out in the Indian equivalent of Sunday-go-to-meeting clothes. A signal was sounded. Soon the villagers were filing into the main lodge.

Bowie's head snapped up. "I just noticed. They're free."

"Who?"

"The blacks. Their shackles are gone. The Indians must have done it to make better time on the trek here." Bowie was pleased. "It will make our job that much easier. I'll go for them while you fetch your partner."

"What about Arlo?"

"What about him?"

"We can't let them do it. Not even to Kastner."

"Listen to yourself. The man is scum. He tried to kill Sam. He stole the Africans right out from under me. I don't give a damn whether they eat him boiled or roasted. Neither should you."

"It's just not right," Davy insisted.

"There's a lot about this world of ours that isn't right, Tennessee. People suffer. People starve. People are treated like dirt by those who think an accident of birth makes them better than everyone else."

"We can't do much about all that. But we're here. Now. And we can do something to help Kastner."

Bowie faced him. "*You* help him if you want. I won't lift a finger. And don't bother pointing out the error of my ways. I'm not much on turning the other cheek. Never have been. Maybe one day it will be the death of me, but if so, so be it."

"I'll try and save Kastner then."

"Don't take this personal, but you're a damned fool if you do."

Davy tried to make light of his decision. "Heck. If I had a dollar for every damn fool stunt I've pulled, I'd be governor."

Bowie slowly rose. "It's time. The last of them just went into the council lodge." The frontiersman thrust a hand out.

"What's this for?"

"In case either of us are maggot bait by morning. It's been a privilege knowing you. You've stirred things inside me I thought were buried for good. Feelings about what's right and what's wrong."

Touched, Davy shook hands. "Just don't get carried away by it. Or next thing you know, you *will* go into politics. And folks will blame me for bringing you to ruin."

The big knife streaked from its sheath. James Bowie winked, then glided off like a panther, toward the pen.

Davy produced the tomahawk and followed the taller man to the tree line. There, they parted, Davy to swing north, then east. The warrior who had been behind the long lodge was no longer there. A rosy glow spilled from a narrow rectangular opening six feet up on the rear wall. Not so much a window, Davy reckoned, as for ventilation. Tendrils of smoke wafted from it. The Indians were engaged in a singsong chant, and someone was sobbing.

Davy crept from concealment. A strange noise from around the northeast corner caused him to spin and hike the tomahawk. But no one appeared. Puzzled, he dashed to the corner. The man he loved like a brother was locked in mortal combat with the warrior who had been on guard.

Flavius was on his knees, the warrior's hands clamped on his neck. Bit by bit, he was having the life strangled from his body. Flavius blamed himself for being a shade too slow when they confronted one another. The Indian had swung his war club, but Flavius had skipped under it and buried his knuckles in the man's gut. It had been like hitting a sack of rocks. Before Flavius could say "Jack Frost," the man was on him, fingers of banded steel about to crush his jugular like so much putty.

Flavius thought his time had come. He couldn't breathe. His vision swam. He was so disoriented, he thought that he saw Davy rear up behind the warrior, thought he saw the tomahawk glint dully. Then the world blinked black and he was falling. Or rather, sinking like a feather.

So this is what it feels like to be dead, Flavius mused. A sense of great peace came over him. Lassitude rendered him as weak as a newborn infant. He had the sensation of drifting, like a cloud. Oddly, he was not scared. He had a conviction that at any second he would open his eyes and gaze on the golden spires of Heaven.

A stiff wind buffeted his cloud. Flavius wanted to cling to something, but there was nothing to hold onto. He was worried that he would fall, that he would plummet all the way back down to Earth and be shattered into a million pieces.

"Flavius? Can you hear me?"

The voice sounded remarkably like Davy's, but that

couldn't be. Davy couldn't be in Heaven; he was still alive. "Are you an angel?" Flavius said thickly. "Come to take me to my reward?"

"Hush, you jughead! Do you want the Indians to hear?"

Indians? Surely there wouldn't be Indians in the Hereafter! Flavius opened his eyes. Above him was his friend's face, etched with concern. "How in tarnation did you get to Heaven?" Flavius asked. "Did those Karankawas take you by surprise?"

"I hate to disappoint you," Davy whispered, "but I'm a likelier candidate for a pitchfork than I am a halo and wings." Leaning down, he grinned. "Besides, you're not shed of this life yet."

"Huh?" Flavius rose onto his elbows. Beside him lay the warrior who had been strangling him, the Irishman's tomahawk embedded in his skull. "Oh. You saved me."

"Don't sound so upset or next time I won't." Davy pulled his friend up off the ground, then placed a foot on the dead Indian's face and wrenched the tomahawk out. "Are you up to running?"

"Just you try and lose me," Flavius bantered louder than he meant to. Appalled by his lapse, he covered his mouth and listened for an outcry. All he heard was chanting. In the distance a bird screeched.

Davy shoved Liz against Flavius's chest. "Take her. My pistols are caked with crud or I'd give them to you."

"What will you use?"

"I can protect myself, don't you worry." Davy hefted the tomahawk, then turned and sped on around the lodge. Stopping under the opening, he rose onto the tips of his toes. The scene he beheld was like something out of the dawn of time, from an age before the first white man set foot on the North American continent.

The Indians were divided into three groups. In a wide aisle in the middle were the men, arrayed in twelve rows, facing their leader, who stood on a raised dais at the rear. Along the right wall were the women, dressed in short skirts, their hands primly clasped. Along the left wall were the children, meekly observing the ceremony.

Two outsiders were present. Tied to thick posts in front of the dais were Arlo Kastner and the black woman. Both had been stripped bare. It was Arlo who sobbed nonstop, his cheeks slick with tears.

The chief had both arms upraised, a knife in each hand. He led the chant, reciting a ritual that must have been as old as the human race itself.

Between the posts and the front row of warriors yawned a gaping black hole A pit. How deep, or what arcane purpose it served, was a mystery.

At a gesture from the gray-haired elder, two muscular warriors advanced. Both, Davy noted, gave the pit a wide berth. From within it came loud rustling.

"What the devil is in there?"

Flavius had pressed an eye to the opening's lower edge. The question had risen unbidden, but he'd had the presence of mind to keep his voice low enough so only the Irishman heard. He shuddered to think that but for the grace of God, he'd be tied to one of those poles instead of the river rat.

Davy noted that torches lined the walls; then he began to turn, to go help Bowie. He paused when the leader descended the dais and solemnly walked over to Kastner. The chanting reached a crescendo, every man, woman, and child taking part. As the tribal leader halted, it died.

The only sound now was Arlo's weeping. Sniffling, he said, "Please! I don't want to die! Spare me and I'll get you anything you want. Guns. Axes. Blankets. You name it. I can get it. Honest."

The leader touched the tip of a blade to the riverrat's forehead, to Arlo's chest, to both shoulders.

Davy tore himself from the tableau. He had to prevent what

was going to happen next. But he had only taken a stride when a blood-curdling wail prickled his scalp. He looked back inside.

Arlo Kastner had not suffered unduly. The hilt of one of the ceremonial knives jutted from his chest, a scarlet rivulet flowing to his navel. All the Indians were smiling, and they resumed chanting as the leader gripped the hilt firmly and sliced from side to side.

Davy could not quite see what the man was doing. The African woman could, though, and her features mirrored unbridled fright. Within moments the chief finished and stepped to the right to wave aloft his trophy.

It was Arlo's heart!

After giving a knife to each of the two warriors, the leader held the organ in his palms overhead. Intoning an incantation, he moved toward the pit, blood dripping onto his headdress and shoulders.

Flavius had stopped watching. He could only abide so much. The image of that still-beating heart would linger in his memory for as long as he lived.

At the pit's rim the chief halted. Again he appealed to whatever gods his people worshiped while the rustling grew louder and louder. Then he tossed the heart into the hole. A rumbling growl filled the lodge, and as if it were prearranged, the people raised their voices in a new song.

Davy nudged Flavius and sped to the pen. The blacks were not in it. They were gathered near an open gate at the southwest corner. Of Bowie there was no sign. Confused, Davy glanced toward the front of the lodge. James and one of the Africans were at the wide door, but they did not linger. Pivoting, they raced to the gate, the wrath of the Almighty crackling on Bowie's brow.

"Did you see? Did you see what was done to Arlo?"

"I saw."

"We can't let them do the same to that woman. We're going to save her if we can."

"Twenty-one of us against a hundred?"

"We'll have the element of surprise. If we hit them hard and fast, we can cut her loose and be out of there before they mount a counterattack."

Flavius couldn't believe what he was hearing. "It's suicide," he whispered. "You'll get all of us killed."

"Don't come, if you'd rather not," Bowie said with no ill will. "She's my responsibility anyway. All of them are."

"How do they feel about it?" Davy asked.

Bowie had no need to answer. Every last African had stepped to the fence. The poles were held in place by loops of cord, which were quickly severed by the big knife Bowie had lent a curly-haired man with a thin bone through his nose.

Flavius was dismayed. "Poles against war clubs? You won't stand a prayer."

"That's just it," Bowie responded. "Didn't you notice? Most of the warriors don't have their clubs with them. Maybe it's forbidden. So we *do* have a prayer." He accepted his knife from the husky black. "This is N'tembo. He's from the Congo. That woman about to have her heart cut out is his wife."

N'tembo could not hide his misery.

James Bowie stared at the two Tennesseans. "So what will it be? Are you in or out?"

Davy felt Flavius's eyes bore into him. His friend would do whatever he did. And he must make up his mind quickly. The chanting had grown louder. Anyone with half a brain would refuse, but as Davy's oldest sister, Betsy, always liked to joke, when the brains in his family were passed out, he was off coon hunting. "Count us in."

Chapter Eleven

Flavius Harris wanted to scream. Not from pain. Or from fear. He wanted to scream because he was mad enough to chew rocks. Mad that after all he had been through on behalf of the Africans, after being captured and nearly strangled to death in an attempt to save their lives, they were going to get themselves wiped out anyway. And him along with them.

Davy was as much to blame. They were partners. Whatever the Irishman did, Flavius would do. Davy knew this. So by agreeing to help Bowie and the blacks, Davy was putting both their lives in peril without even bothering to ask his opinion.

It was unfair. Damned unfair. Flavius felt sorry for the black woman about to be sacrificed, but they had to be practical. They had little hope of saving her. In effect, they were sacrificing themselves. Noble, but needless. They should save the ones they could, and be thankful.

Now Bowie and Davy were jogging toward the front of the medicine lodge. Flavius dogged their steps, regretting every one. Nervously, he fingered the rifle, and made a mental note. If *anyone* ever again showed up on his doorstep and asked him to go on a gallivant, he'd sic his dogs on them.

Davy Crockett listened to the swelling volume of the chant, and prayed they would not be too late. A peek past the jamb revealed the leader was back on the dais, going through the same ritual as before with a new set of knives. Soon he was would descend and carve the poor woman's heart out.

"Ready?" James Bowie whispered.

Davy glanced at the torches that lined both sides of the building, at the dry brush and limbs used in the construction of the walls. "I have a brainstorm," he mentioned. "You go for the woman. I'll see to it that the Indians have something else to worry about besides us."

Flavius did not like the sound of that. His friend was going to do something that would compound the danger for the two of them. He was sure of it. Yet he said softly, "I'm ready too. I'll be right behind you, Davy."

Crockett shifted. "No, you won't. Someone has to cover us. You hold back right here. When we have the woman and we're on our way out, do what you can to keep those warriors off our backs."

Flavius was overjoyed. He'd be the safest—barring something unforeseen. Then a suspicion came over him, and he whispered, "Why me? You're not doing this to spare me, are you?"

"Heavens, no," Davy fibbed. "You have Liz, is all. I have the tomahawk. Can I help it I'm a little better at close-in fighting?"

The Irishman was a *lot* better, but Flavius did not quibble. "Oh. In that case, you can count on me."

James Bowie shoved his own rifle at the portly Tennessean. "You might as well have mine too. And my pistols, while we're at it."

Flavius felt like a walking armory. The extra-long gun he leaned against the wall. The pistols he slid under his belt, but loosely. "Be careful in there," he cautioned. "If you need me to come in, just give a holler."

"Will do." Davy saw the chief stride to the stairs. They could not delay any longer. Looking at James, he whispered, "Do you want to do the honors, or should I?"

"She's my responsibility," the tall frontiersman stressed. Then he did a strange thing. He raised the big knife to his lips and kissed the blade. Next he winked at Davy, motioned at N'tembo, and charged. He did not whoop or bellow or roar. Silently, grimly, he crossed the open space, and was in among the last row of warriors, slashing and hacking, before they knew what had hit them.

N'tembo and the Africans were right at his side, wielding their poles in a frenzy, clubbing, butting, pounding. Over a dozen shaggy figures were writhing on the ground when a woman screeched like a hawk, drawing all eyes to the melee. The warriors in the front ranks whirled to join the battle as other women screamed and children wailed.

Davy angled to the right-hand wall. Seizing the first torch, he yanked it off its wooden pedestal and pressed the burning head to the dry wall. Immediately, the brush and limbs ignited. Hungry flames spread with astounding rapidity, smoke spewing outward.

Davy dashed to the next torch and repeated the procedure. He'd counted on the Indians being too preoccupied with Bowie and the Africans to pay much attention to him, but he'd miscalculated. As he thrust the second torch at the wall, a lanky warrior sprang at him from behind. Spidery arms wrapped around his chest. Simultaneously, several women rushed over to help.

Davy swung his whole weight to the left, waving the torch in front of him. It stopped the women in their tracks. With his other hand he swung the tomahawk down and back. He felt it sink into yielding flesh, heard a cry in his ear. The warrior's grip slackened. A mighty heave, and Davy broke

146

loose. Spinning, he whipped the tomahawk in a short slash that opened the man's throat from ear to ear.

The women renewed their assault, joined by five or six more. Short stone knives had blossomed from under their skirts. Davy used the torch to hold them at bay. But he could not reach the next pedestal. And he needed to set more of the wall afire quickly, in order to forestall a massacre of his allies.

Suddenly, a black woman was at his elbow, her pole held in a wide grip, her feet spread in a wide stance. She looked at him and smiled. Then she flew into the Indian women, her pole flashing right and left, showing no fear of the knives that cut at her like claws. Single-handed, she drove the Indian women steadily backward.

Davy flung the sputtering torch at a wild-eyed Indian who was holding her ground. Tomahawk uplifted, he leaped toward the next pedestal. Another woman, retreating, slipped and fell. He could have split her head like a ripe melon. But he didn't. He had never slain a female. God willing, he never would.

The lithe African had felled four foes. Her pole was a dazzling blur, its length enabling her to keep the Indian women from getting close enough to effectively use their blades.

Davy reached the torch, ripped it from its roost, and applied the crackling flames to the building. A quarter of the wall was ablaze now, the fire spreading to the roof too rapidly to be contained. Thick, roiling smoke spread outward just as swiftly, engulfing Africans and Indians alike.

Bedlam reigned. Children cried and yelled. Indian women frantically sought to reach their offspring. The warriors continued to battle Bowie and the Africans, who were slowly but inevitably pushing toward the post and the bound woman.

Not all the warriors had left their war clubs at home. Enough were armed to pose a serious challenge. Struggling to the forefront, they engaged the blacks in fierce combat.

In the thick of it was James Bowie, his big knife weaving

a glittering tapestry of death. Holding the hilt as if it were a sword, he slashed and hacked and chopped, felling all those who opposed him.

Davy saw the tribe's leader approach the woman at the stake. Sacrificial knives aloft, he moved with solemn, measured tread, unruffled by the conflict, unaffected by the bedlam. Bowie and the Africans could not possibly reach her in time to save her. So Davy, taking a long bound, scattered the Indian women with a wide swing of his tomahawk. Then, as stinging smoke swirled around him, he sprinted to the captive's rescue.

To reach the post Davy had to skirt the pit. Already wispy gray tendrils were wafting into it, agitating the inhabitant. A booming bellow resounded. Davy, glancing down, felt his blood change to ice.

The pit was ten feet deep, approximately thirty wide. It was littered with white bones, mostly *human* bones, and with skulls that grinned stupidly, as if happy to be dead. A noxious odor rose from the hole, the foulest of smells, a stench putrid and obscene. Davy had to hold his breath to keep from retching.

Sprawled amidst the sea of bones was an alligator, the most enormous of its kind that the Irishman had ever seen or heard tell of. A gigantic creature, fully twenty feet from the end of its snout to the tip of its tail. A monster twice as wide as any gator ever born. A beast that should not exist and yet did, much like the Indians themselves. It saw the Tennessean. Its maw gaped and it lunged at the rim, rising impossibly high despite its bulk, its teeth gnashing within a few feet of Davy's legs.

Davy had heard that gators could jump much higher than most folks believed possible. Here was living proof. In pure reflex he darted aside.

Then he was at the posts. The two assistants rushed him, one unarmed, but the other brandishing a heavy club upraised to cave in his skull. The elder stood in front of the woman, waving the sacrificial knives. At any moment he would bury one in her unprotected bosom.

Davy swung a terrific blow at the warrior with the club. But the man parried, rotated, and came at him in a whirlwind. Davy held firm, giving as good as he got, blocking, countering, unhurt but unable to inflict any damage. The unarmed warrior circled, seeking an opening to exploit.

Over at the post, the elder had stopped waving the long knives. Slowly hiking an arm, he prepared for the killing stroke.

Desperate straits called for desperate measures. Suddenly tucking at the knees, Davy sheared the tomahawk into his adversary's left thigh. The warrior with the club roared and backpedaled, blood spraying. Spinning, Davy took two steps and launched his weapon in an overhand toss at the elder. The unarmed warrior bellowed a warning and pounced, but the deed was done.

Wreathed by sinuous fingers of smoke, the sacrificial knife surged downward. But it never sank into its intended victim. For at that instant the tomahawk thudded into the elder's chest, to the left of the sternum. Jolted, the man clutched at the handle. Grimacing, he did a slow pirouette, and lay feebly kicking and plucking at the weapon that had laid him low.

Davy had saved the black woman, but in so doing he had let down his own guard. The unarmed warrior slammed into him and drove him rearward, into a choking, blinding cloud of smoke. He punched the man's back and shoulders, then absorbed a knee meant for his groin but which struck his inner thigh. Inexplicably, the warrior did not let go. Legs pumping, the man kept driving him farther and farther backward.

Away from the sacrifice, Davy reasoned. Enough was enough, though. Davy pivoted, hooked an arm under the warrior's shoulder, and slung the man as if he were a sack of potatoes. It was an old wrestling trick, honed during bouts at

149

church socials and the like where friendly matches were the order of the day.

The man went flying. But his fingers wrapped around Davy's wrist, clamping like a vise, and Davy was pulled off balance and stumbled a few more feet.

The smoke was thick enough to cut with an ax. The Tennessean braced his legs, heard a squawk. Abruptly, he was tugged downward. Gritting his teeth, he stopped himself. It was a short respite. The warrior screamed. Then there was a bone-wrenching yank that no man could resist. Davy's feet left the earth, and he was falling. He tensed for the impact, puzzled when it did not occur. He fell much farther than he should have.

Only when his shoulder crashed down with excruciating force and agony eclipsed all other sensations did the terrible truth dawn.

He was in the alligator pit.

Flavius Harris was a bundle of frayed nerves. He watched as Bowie and the Africans, in a compact wedge, plowed through the Indians like a scythe through grain. He saw Davy and a black woman oppose a knot of she-cats. Then his friend raced toward the tall posts.

As fate would have it, when Davy needed him the most, a swirling bank of smoke drifted completely across the lodge, shrouding everything and everyone. Flavius could no longer see Bowie, no longer see the Africans. To his consternation, he could not see Davy either, and he moved into the doorway for a better look. Out of the cloud rushed a warrior, a war club gripped in bloody hands.

Flavius shot him dead. Snatching a pistol, he cocked it and moved a few yards to the right. "Davy! Davy! Where are you?"

The uproar smothered his shout. Other figures assumed substance in the murky veil. He aimed the flintlock but did not fire, not when he discovered how small the figures were. Seven, eight, nine children fled past, boys and girls alike, some crying.

"Davy! Answer me!"

Flavius swatted at the smoke. A losing proposition, since the cloud grew denser by the moment and had expanded from the floor to the ceiling. He imagined that being in it would be like having one's head dunked in pea soup.

So that Bowie and Davy would have some idea of where the entrance was, Flavius commenced hollering, "This way! Over here!"

More Indians sped into the night, woman and children in a panic. A wounded man was next, limping and bleeding from a ragged gash above an ear. The warrior made no threatening moves, so Flavius allowed him to leave.

"Davy! James! Light a shuck! Hurry!"

Two women stumbled on out, coughing violently, tears pouring from smoke-seared eyes.

"Davy! For God's sake, answer me!"

Flavius could not say which was worse; the waiting, or not knowing whether the Irishman and Bowie were still alive. He scooted back to the doorway, planning to hold his ground no matter what, but a screeching, sobbing mob of children and women drove him outside.

Smoke poured from the opening. Flavius probed the acrid fog as more members of the tribe staggered out into the darkness, many gasping, most so blinded they did not notice him. He yelled a few more times, and had about despaired of being answered when a new knot of hurrying silhouettes materialized. In the lead was a tall warrior. Flavius centered the pistol, waiting to squeeze the trigger until the tall one was so close he couldn't possibly miss.

The smoke parted briefly, revealing James Bowie and the Africans. The naked woman who was to be sacrificed clung to her husband, N'tembo.

151

"We did it!" Bowie exclaimed. "Let's cut out for the swamp while we still have the advantage."

No encouragement was needed. Flavius assumed that when Bowie said "we," it included his best friend. Grabbing the rifle he had leaned against the wall, he handed it to the broad-shouldered woodsman, noticing as he did that Bowie's big knife was scarlet from tip to hilt.

They ran, Flavius glad to bid the village good-bye. After the stinging confines of the lodge, the muggy air was like a blast of chill wind. It invigorated him. He had no difficulty keeping pace with Bowie.

Frenzied cries and the crackle of flames dwindled in the distance. Flavius hoped the fire would occupy the Indians for quite a while, preferably all night. By dawn the village would be miles distant, escape assured.

Bowie did not call a halt until they reached a clearing hemmed by briars, where they caught their breath and took stock. Flavius counted eleven Africans left, three severely hurt. Seven lives, then, had been lost to save the one woman. *Had it been worth it?* Only the Africans could say, and to judge from their weary smiles, they thought so. Hunkering down, he set to reloading Liz.

"Where's Crockett?" asked Bowie.

Flavius, about to uncap his powder horn, glanced at Bowie. "What?" he asked, even though he had heard the question clearly.

"Where's Davy?"

"He's not with us?"

"Do you see him?"

No, Flavius did not. Anxiety twisted his vitals. "Oh, God."

"I lost track of him early on," Bowie explained. "I had my hands full staying alive." Irritated, he smacked a fist against his other palm. "Damn it to hell! I should have paid more attention. I just figured you would have said something if he wasn't with us."

"And I figured he was all along," Flavius said. "With the blacks, or bringing up the rear." Which was the natural thing for Davy to do. Still, Flavius *should* have checked, not taken it for granted.

Bowie swore. "He must not have made it out. Too bad. He was a rare one, that Irishman. Too many men I've met aren't worth their weight in flour. He was worth his weight in gold."

Flavius wholeheartedly agreed, but the compliment did not dull the awful ravaging pang that seared his chest. At long last what he had long dreaded had taken place. He groaned softly, weakness creeping into his legs so that he had to sit.

Images of Davy paraded through his head, of the time back home, at a local tavern, when Davy won a bet by quaffing a pitcher of ale nonstop; of a dance they had gone to where Davy spent the whole night cheek to cheek with Elizabeth, as much in love as any man had ever been; and of a hunt one autumn, during which the dogs had flushed a she-bear that Davy spared because he heard cubs bawling in a thicket. Those three incidents pretty well summed the man up. "I'm going back."

"Like hell you are."

Flavius willed his legs to straighten. "I have to. It's my fault we didn't notice sooner. Maybe he's still alive. Maybe those savages are fixing to sacrifice him like they did Arlo."

"You would be throwing your life away. I can't allow that."

"You can't stop me," Flavius declared.

Bowie scratched his chin, deep in thought, and took several steps. "I'm as much to blame as you. By rights, I should go back too. But these Africans will never make it out of the swamp on their own. For their sake, I have to stay." He stared at a man whose shoulder had been shattered by a war club. "As for Davy, he knew the risks. If he is alive, if those cannibals have him, we couldn't reach the village in time."

Flavius lifted Liz. He would reload while on the trail. "We don't know that for sure. I've got to find out, one way or the other."

"I was afraid you would say that."

A mallet fist connected with Flavius's jaw. His surprise lasted only as long as it took him to hit the ground. Then he knew nothing.

Flavius was ten years old again. He held a thin limb he had trimmed and sharpened to a point. In a pond ahead, a bull-frogs croaked. His pa was partial to frog's legs, so Flavius was going to treat his father to a heaping helping for supper. Or his ma would, once Flavius had speared a few. He snuck through high weeds to the shore. At the water's edge was a large male. He could tell by the ears. Males had bigger, darker ears than females.

Since sudden movement would spook it, Flavius slowly drew back his spear. The frog moved its legs, bobbing like a cork. Flavius held still to fool it into thinking he was harmless. Presently, he was ready. About to throw, he coiled—and was roughly shaken by his shoulder, as if by an invisible hand. He tried to shrug it off, but it gripped harder and shook with more vigor. The bullfrog promptly dived.

"No!" Flavius declared. The same invisible hand clamped over his mouth to stifle another outcry. He struggled to speak, and suddenly his eyes were open and he saw James Bowie and a ring of black faces, and realized the hand was Bowie's.

"Not so loud, friend. We're being hunted."

Flavius sat up. They were not in the clearing anymore. To the east a pink tinge framed the horizon. Its significance stupefied him. "I've been unconscious all night? It's dawn?" Shoving upright, he scanned the lush swampland that now surrounded them. "Where are we? How far from the village?"

Bowie was gazing to the north. "About fifteen miles,

would be my guess. We didn't stop to rest once all night."

"How did I—?" Flavius began.

"How else? We carried you in pairs, taking turns." Bowie nodded at a makeshift litter built from uneven limbs interwoven with slim vines. "I would have woke you sooner, but I knew you'd raise a fuss over Crockett."

The reminder lanced a hot poker through Flavius. Forgetting himself, he grasped the front of the bigger man's shirt. "Damn you! You had no right! I might have saved him!"

Bowie did not lift a finger to defend himself. "You want to pound me to a pulp, don't you? But I'd do the same if we had it to do all over again."

"*Why?* I thought you liked him."

"I do. We were kindred souls, Davy and I. So I did what he would have done, and saved you from yourself. But if you need to hit me, go right ahead."

A powerful hankering to do just that came over Flavius. He balled his hand and raised it, but he could not quite bring himself to smash his knuckles into Bowie's face. "I should. I honestly and truly should." Yet would it be fair when James had only had his best interests at heart? He was spared from having to make up his mind by faint sounds. Yipping, such as coyotes would do, only harsher, and more strident.

"Do you hear?" Bowie asked. "They're on our trail. They'll be on us shortly after sunrise unless I miss my guess."

"Then why are we standing here jawing?"

The Africans were exhausted, haggard. Those who had been wounded were unable to walk without aid. Yet they plodded on, tapping into a reservoir of stamina that lent vitality to their flagging limbs.

Pools had to be negotiated. Bushes that clung to a person's limbs like living wire. Treacherous soil that buckled under a man's weight. It seemed to Flavius that Bowie was rashly leading them through the worst section of swamp there was, and he commented as much.

"See that small hill yonder?" the frontiersman responded, pointing at a mound that in Tennessee would be too small to earn the distinction. "On the other side is dry ground. Not much, a couple of acres, but enough for us to make a stand. And trees for cover."

"Sorry I doubted you."

The yipping grew louder. It made Flavius think of the coon hunts he had been on, of the baying of the hounds as they closed in on their quarry. *Was this how raccoons felt? Scared? Trapped? Helpless?* He had always thought it great fun, but from this day forth he would view it in a whole new light.

Some of the Africans had stopped and were arguing. Bowie went down the line to learn the cause. Meanwhile, the demonic yipping of their pursuers took on a new, excited note. The Indians realized their prey was near, and were coming on faster.

Flavius was anxious to get over the hill, to have solid ground under his feet again. It mystified him when Bowie and the other blacks resumed hiking. A wounded man, propped on a pole, had been left on a hummock. "What gives?" he asked when James rejoined him.

"Mokole can't go any further. He's too weak, too sick. Blood poisoning, I suspect."

"So we let those cannibals butcher him?"

Bowie had lengthened his stride and did not look back. "Mokole wanted it this way. He'd be a burden, delay us. And he won't last much longer anyway. So he's going to wait there and try to slow them down. For our sakes."

"He'd do that for you? For someone who was going to sell him into slavery?"

"Not for me. Or even for you." Bowie motioned at the rest of the Africans. "For them. He's sacrificing himself to gain them an extra minute or two. We'll need it.''

The race was close, and proved Bowie right. They had just crested the hill when an exultant medley of war whoops signaled the end of the valiant man on the hummock. On their last legs, the Africans stumbled into the trees, then turned at bay. They had gone so long without nourishment and adequate rest that for most it took a monumental effort simply to stay on their feet.

''Any last prayers you want to make?'' James Bowie inquired. ''Now is the time.''

Flavius faced the hill. Thronged on top of it, crowded together like a pack of wild dogs eager to taste blood, was the war party.

Chapter Twelve

Davy Crockett froze as a huge shape loomed in front of him. The giant alligator had heard him strike the ground, but thanks to the thick, swirling smoke, the monster could not find him.

Davy could see part of the gator, though. At the bottom of the pit was a layer of clear air, a gap of five or six inches. The reptile's enormous feet were plainly visible. So was part of its tail, which suddenly flicked toward Davy as the creature turned. Clattering over bones, the sinuous batting ram sent a skull tumbling, and came within spitting distance of Davy's face. The Tennessean pressed against the side of the pit, coiled to leap should it swing any closer. As powerful as it was, it could easily crush his ribs or break an arm.

Above the pit, bedlam ruled. Men roared, screamed, died.

Suddenly there was a loud thump, so close that Davy jumped. Bile rose in his gorge. The warrior who had tried to push him into the pit was no longer a threat. The upper half of the man's body flopped like a fish out of water, the mouth jerking in spasms. Below the waist only shredded flesh and crushed bone remained; the gator had bitten him in half.

Davy peered upward. He could not rely on Bowie or Flavius to save his bacon since neither had seen him fall in. It was doubtful *anyone* had, friend or foe alike. He was on his own. Whether he lived or died depended solely on how resourceful he was.

The pit rim was ten feet overhead. With a running start he might be able to jump and grab hold. But that wasn't feasible. The gator would be in his way.

Davy rose onto his hands and knees, careful not to disturb any bones. It was highly unlikely the reptile would hear so slight a noise, what with the tumult in the lodge, but Davy had learned long ago never to take anything for granted.

Drifting smoke eddied like an ocean current. Bending, Davy noted the position of the alligator's body, particularly the tail, then circled in the opposite direction, staying low. He placed each foot lightly. A rumbling grunt brought him to a stop. Crouching, he learned that the gator had moved and was now facing him.

Did it know? Davy's mouth went dry. He would give anything to have his tomahawk, but all he had was his butcher knife, which he palmed. It would be like using a toothpick against Leviathan.

The creature's legs slid nearer.

Suddenly the smoke parted for a span of mere seconds. Davy saw the huge beast's scaly head in hideous profile, and a single darkly sinister eye fixed on him in baleful intensity. *Move!* his mind commanded. He did, throwing himself forward as the smoke wreathed the monster again and its tail came sweeping out of the gray gloom to smash against the wall at the exact spot where he had been.

Davy dropped flat. The tail pounded the wall again, then disappeared. He watched the gator's belly slide back and forth and heard loud sniffing. The thing was trying its utmost to

159

find him. And it would eventually. Rising with his stomach flush to the wall, he extended his arms as high as he could. A useless gesture, since the rim was well beyond his reach.

Meanwhile, the battle above raged on. Davy thought he heard Flavius yell. A child cried hysterically. A man groaned in anguish.

The Tennessean crouched again to keep track of the gator. An instant later a *thud* announced a new arrival. A warrior had fallen in, or been pushed. The man rolled onto his belly, realized where he was, and screeched in mortal panic. As well he should. The alligator had pivoted toward him, bones crunching under its massive bulk. Scrambling back against the side, the warrior grew rigid as the behemoth stalked closer.

Get out of there! Davy wanted to shout. But the Indian would not understand, and it would focus the gator's attention on himself.

Only part of the man's legs could be seen below the smoke. Davy could only imagine the warrior's expression as the reptile drew nearer and nearer.

The alligator halted. The man's legs shook, and it seemed as if he were about to bolt, when there was a pulpy ripping sound, like that of an orange being squished. The man swayed, his torso tilting outward. Onto the bones spilled a headless corpse, pumping blood.

The smoke was growing thicker; the air at the bottom was growing less. Soon there would be only smoke, and Davy would have no way of seeing the gator. He'd be completely at its mercy.

As if that were not danger enough, a rain of burning embers from on high warned the Tennessean the roof was now ablaze. It was only a matter of time before whole sections came crashing down—some into the pit. If the gator didn't get him, the smoke would, and if both of those failed, he might very well be smashed to bits or burned to a crisp.

What to do? Another rain of debris added urgency when it provoked the alligator into a fierce upheaval. Bellowing and lashing its tail, the creature turned this way and that. Perhaps in the depths of its dim brain it recognized its life was threatened. A will to survive propelled it against the pit wall, where it clawed at the earth in a frenzy, dislodging big chunks and digging a furrow. Either it was smart enough to sense the futility of its actions, or it grew tired, but in any event it presently subsided and was still.

From the position of the belly and tail, Davy deduced the gator was bent upward, with half its body against the pit wall. An insane idea spurred him into slinking toward the center. Once there, he moved closer to the creature, avoiding bones prone to break and give him away.

The alligator did not move.

Davy was near enough to touch the tail if he were so inclined when the reptile growled and grumbled like a black bear fresh out of hibernation. The smoke was getting to it. Or the flames, which now shot downward from the inferno that had once been the roof. The heat was withering; the temperature had climbed twenty or thirty degrees, and it was blistery hot.

Davy was sweating something awful. He wiped a sleeve across his brow while inching closer. What he contemplated doing might get him killed, but he would rather die *doing something* than sit there and meekly wait for eternity to claim him. He slid the butcher knife into its sheath, wiped his palms on his pants, and was ready.

The alligator stirred. It began to slide to the ground. Davy had heartbeats in which to put his plan into effect, and he did so by hurtling himself at the gator, grabbing hold, and shimming up the monster's back as he would scale a knotty pine. Bumps and thick scales gave him some purchase, but it was still slippery, still like trying to climb a grassy slope slick

161

with moisture. He reached the hindquarters, and shimmied higher.

Belatedly, the creature exploded into motion. Its whole body canted to the left and its neck twisted as it sought to snap him in twain. But alligator necks were stout and short, too short to bend very far.

Davy dug his fingers in and levered higher. Another dozen inches or so and he would be high enough. Suddenly the alligator bucked like a wild mustang, almost throwing him off. At the same time, the animal started to slide back down the wall.

It was now or never! Davy launched himself at the rim. He could not see it. He had no idea how far he had to spring, or if he was high enough to reach it. But salvation was there, somewhere. His fingers splayed wide, he flailed at the smoke, seeking purchase.

A blow from below catapulted him head over heels. A blow so powerful, his chest felt as if he had been split wide. His senses swam. An impact equally devastating left him stunned and weak. He did not know where he was, whether still in the pit or outside of it.

Smoke seeped into his nostrils, into his mouth. His lungs were seared as if by twin swords. Gasping for air that was not there, he crawled toward he knew-not-what, praying it wasn't toward the gator.

Davy bumped into something. Recoiling, he waited for the crunch of iron jaws. When he was not attacked, he probed through the smoke. The object was hard and round, like a tree trunk, only it was not a tree trunk. It was one of the posts to which sacrifices were tied. Leaning against it, he slowly rose.

The alligator was raising a ruckus. From the front of the building came shouts and cries in jumbled chorus.

Davy wondered whose post it was, Arlo's or the woman's? No one was bound to it, so he reasoned it was the one the black woman had been tied to and she had been set free. Bowie had done it.

It was high time he got out of there as well. A halting step brought him to a sprawled body. His left foot snagged and he tripped. The body cushioned his fall, and his hand, outflung, slid across a buckskin shirt dampened by blood and made contact with a hardwood hilt. The handle to his cherished tomahawk.

Davy yanked the weapon out, held it close to his chest a moment, then staggered on. It was becoming harder and harder to breathe. Covering his mouth, he breathed shallowly to avoid inhaling more smoke.

He knew where he was now, and what he had to do. When he bumped into the dais, he roved to the right until he located the stairs, and climbed. The higher he went, the worse the smoke became. Bent at the waist, he hastened another fifteen to twenty feet, and his outstretched fingers brushed the rear wall.

Roving his hand in wide arcs, Davy soon found the rectangular ventilation hole. Standing directly under it, he lit into the wall with vinegar and vim, chopping and hacking as if his very life depended on the outcome. Which it did.

The wall was thick, but the brush and limbs were brittle. The tomahawk made short shrift of them, biting deep with every stroke. The *thunk-thunk-thunk* was loud enough to attract interest, but he doubted warriors would investigate. The Indians had their hands full with Bowie and the Africans, or with helping to save the women and children.

His eyes stung horribly. His lungs were on the verge of collapse. But Davy did not give up. Quitters were natural-born losers, his pa had always said, and he would be damned if anyone would ever include him in that category. He put his shoulders into it, chopping with a vengeance. More wood chips flew, but not nearly enough. He *must* open a large enough hole before he succumbed to the smoke.

It would be close.

Breathing grew even more difficult. Each breath he took was laced with more bitter smoke. His lungs were full of it. They burned terribly, as if filled with acid. Somewhere or other, he recollected being told that in most fires, smoke claimed more victims than flames. He inhaled and held it, thinking that would reduce the torment, but it didn't. The pain grew worse.

Davy was weakening. Every muscle in his arms ached. His shoulders throbbed. His head pounded as if to the beat of a heavy hammer. Both legs trembled, his knees on the verge of buckling. Only through supreme force of will did he stay upright.

I must keep swinging! Davy railed at himself. *I must keep chopping or I will die. I'll never get to see my beloved wife again, to tell her how truly sorry I am for being as thick-skinned as an ox and as thickheaded as a mule. I should never have gone on this gallivant. Never have given in to my urge to always see what lay over the next horizon.* Not for nothing was there an old saying that "curiosity killed the cat."

His lungs were on fire. He could not breathe without being racked by exquisite agony. His arms were leaden; no, they were heavier than lead. Each blow was a strain.

Davy swung again. *Thwack!* His swings were losing their force. Once more he struck, but it was not enough. He did not need to see the opening he had made to know it wasn't big enough. Tears streamed from his eyes, his nose was running, and his throat felt as if someone had poured scalding-hot oil down it. He had done his best, but it wasn't good enough.

In despair, the Irishman drew back the tomahawk for a final try. His legs had other ideas, and he crumpled, throwing both hands out against the wall to brace himself. Instead of holding him up, the weakened wall crumpled.

Davy blacked out. He could not say how long he was unconscious, but when he revived he was dumfounded to find the firmament sprinkled by stars. He lay amid broken pieces of the collapsed rear wall. Ominous crackling alerted him to the proximity of flames devouring what was left of it.

Like a crab, Davy scuttled toward high grass, sinking gratefully onto his cheek. *The earth felt so cool, so refreshing.* He was happy to be alive. He would be happier yet when they were quit of the village, when Flavius and he were—*Flavius!* Sitting up, Davy listened. The noise of battle had died. Had Harris and Bowie died too?

Shaking his head to clear it, Davy stood. Two thirds of the long lodge was a smoldering ruin, charred debris all that remained. By some miracle small portions had not collapsed even though they were badly damaged. Thick coils of smoke wound skyward. Blackened limbs hissed like riled serpents.

Warily, Davy moved toward the pen. It too had caught fire, and was largely destroyed. Of his friends and the Africans, nary a trace. He padded forward. Then promptly flattened when the night resounded to the drumming of many feet.

Dozens of hairy warriors had jogged from among the conical dwellings. Stripped to their loincloths, armed with spiked clubs, they loped into the swamp.

Davy rose when the last of them was out of sight. Sneaking beyond the smoldering lodge, he spied the women and children in the heart of the village, tending to the wounded. Melancholy gripped one and all, and many wept over those who would rise no more.

Davy felt no remorse. They had brought it on themselves. Without delay he glided into the vegetation. The warriors were making no attempt to be stealthy, indicating that Flavius and the others must be a long way off already. Sprinting, he soon spotted the tail end of the war party. From then on, mile after mile, hour after hour, he always kept them in sight.

He marveled at their ability to track at night. Either they could see in the dark like cats and owls, or they were uncommonly skilled at reading sign by running their hands over the ground. It turned out to be the latter, as he discovered when they paused and several examined a grassy strip.

Fatigue gnawed at him like a beaver at a sapling, but Davy refused to give in to it. His friends would need him in the coming fight. What good he would be, armed only with a tomahawk and knife, was beside the point.

The chase taxed him to his limits. The Indians held to a pace that would tire Apaches, and Apache men could cover seventy miles a day on foot, in the godawful heat of the desert. Or so Texicans asserted.

It was about the middle of the night when Davy glimpsed a glimmer of light to the southeast that had to be the pale glow from a small fire. But who it could be eluded him. Bowie's bunch were traveling due east. That the cannibals hadn't noticed the fire showed how intently they were glued to Bowie's trail.

Davy slowed, cogitating. The fire might belong to whites, but the odds were slim. More probably, it was the camp of Indians belonging to another tribe. And Davy could think of only one other tribe that might be in the area.

Inspiration brought him to a stop. The Irishman stared after the retreating cannibals a bit, then chuckled and sped like the wind toward the distant glow. He had an idea. If it worked, hallelujah! If not, his bleached bones would be proof he was a raving idiot.

Flavius Harris thought of Matilda. His wife, not his rifle. He was sorry he had ever been harsh with her. Sorry he had not been a better husband. And sorriest of all that he had left her to go on Davy's silly gallivant.

The cannibals had fanned out into a crescent and were slowly advancing. Prior to that, for over half an hour, they had stood on the hill, glaring and jabbering.

Flavius had figured the Indians were waiting for the sun to

rise, and he was proven right. As soon as a golden halo crowned the eastern sky, as soon as there was enough light to see clearly, they galvanized to the attack. He glanced at James Bowie. "Well, I reckon this is it."

Bowie wagged that big knife of his, but did not say anything. He did not have to.

"If they were smart, they'd starve us out," Flavius declared. "Let hunger and thirst do the job for them."

"Sometimes an enemy is so fired with hate, they can't wait," Bowie commented. "All they want is blood."

The Africans waited in stoic silence. Some still had poles. Others had found thick limbs to use as clubs. One man held two jagged rocks. They appeared resigned to what was going to occur, resigned and determined to give a good account of themselves. They would all die. It was inevitable. But victory would cost the cannibals dearly.

Flavius tried to swallow, his mouth much too dry. He never thought that he would end his days like this. So far from home. With no kin or close friends to lend comfort. He sighted down Liz at an oncoming savage.

Bowie addressed the Africans in their own dialect. Then, to the Tennessean, he said, "We'll fall back as soon as they rush us. Make them come into the trees after us."

Flavius nodded. It was sound strategy that might gain them a few moments of life. *How precious each moment now seemed!* And how sad that he had always taken them for granted before.

The Indians were seventy yards out. At a yell from a husky warrior, they broke into a run. Not at full speed, not yet. They were pacing themselves, saving their energy for the final sprint.

Another yell, and the cannibals ran faster, in long, loping strides that ate the distance swiftly. They commenced waving their wicked war clubs and whooped in rising bloodlust.

"It was nice making your acquaintance, Harris," James Bowie remarked.

"Same here," Flavius absently responded. There would be no time to reload Liz once he fired. He must fall back, relying on the pistols the frontiersmen had lent him, and when they were empty, he would reverse his grip and club warriors until they brought him low.

The husky cannibal—their new leader—raised an arm and opened his mouth to bellow a third time. He glanced to the right and the left, then behind him at a few who were slower than the rest. Strangely, he broke stride and came to a lurching halt. The bellow was never voiced. His arm drooped, the signal never given.

Those nearest him likewise slowed and stopped. Confusion spread rapidly all along the line, blunting their charge. More and more of them stopped to look back. Within moments all of them were stock still, well shy of the tree line, riveted by the sight that had transfixed their leader.

"I'll be damned!" Bowie exclaimed.

Flavius raised his cheek from Liz, as puzzled as the warriors. He thought his eyes were playing tricks on him, that he could not possibly be seeing what he imagined he was seeing. But it was real.

Davy Crockett was almost to the bottom of the hill. His buckskins clung to him like a second skin, his hair was plastered to his head. He was more exhausted than he could ever recall being, but he did not slow down. He raced straight toward the cannibals. The shock on their faces was priceless. Shock not at his arrival, but at the advent of those who were chasing him.

Davy had fretted he would not arrive in time. Sooner or later the cannibals had been bound to bring his friends to bay, and he had hoped—no, he had prayed—that he would arrive before they were massacred.

Few of the cannibals were paying him any mind. His tomahawk was in one hand, his butcher knife in the other, and he was ready to resist them tooth and nail if they jumped him. But they only had eyes for the newcomers.

Davy shot through a break in their line without mishap. His shoulder blades itched in anticipation of a hurled club, but they let him go. They had a bigger worry. Then he was at the stand, exhausted but elated. He bent over, striving to catch his breath, as Flavius clapped him on the shoulder and James Bowie cackled.

"You're alive, pard! You're alive!"

"Where did you find the Karankawas, Tennessee?"

Davy looked toward the hill. Snake Strangler and thirty painted warriors were arraying themselves to give battle. Between breaths, he gasped, "Oh, I paid them a social visit last night, and they've been chasing me ever since."

Bowie was thunderstruck. "You led them here? On purpose?" He cackled louder. "Dog my cats! If that don't beat bobtail!"

The cannibals were thrusting their clubs at the Karankawas and howling like so many wolves, working themselves into a killing frenzy. Snake Strangler and his war party were almost as noisy, some notching arrows, some drawing knives.

Davy straightened despite his body's protest. "We need to light a shuck now. We'll fetch Sam and head for New Orleans."

"Look!" Flavius said.

The cannibals had charged. Their crescent raged to the hill and started up. War clubs uplifted, yowling at the top of their lungs, they were a human wave no enemy could stop. But the Karankawas tried their utmost. A rain of arrows slashed into the hairy tide, dropping many. A deluge of lances was next, yet still the cannibals surged higher. Snake Strangler and his warriors descended to meet them, the Karankawas holding themselves in regular order. And then ensued a scene few whites had ever been privileged to witness. Indian against

169

Indian, all of them screaming and shrieking as they sought one another's lives with clubs or knives.

At the outset the cannibals had outnumbered the Karankawas, but their ranks had been greatly depleted by the arrows and lances. Now the two sides were about evenly matched. It was man against man, warrior against warrior, brute ferocity and corded sinews pitted against agile frames and keen cunning.

Davy would have sorely liked to see the outcome. Any delay, though, might prove costly. Beckoning, he called out, "Don't stand around gawking!" For Flavius and most of the Africans were doing just that.

All of them were tired. All of them were grimy and sweaty, and some were hurt. Almost all of them had been on their last legs when they reached the trees. Yet now they hurried briskly to the southwest, newfound energy coursing through their veins.

James Bowie glided to Davy's side. "I'm beginning to think your friend is right."

"About what?"

"You really can pull miracles out of that coonskin cap of yours."

Davy chuckled, and remembered his last visit to a local tavern before leaving home. He'd downed more than a few horns of liquor and was feeling no pain. As was the custom, his drinking companions had been boasting of their prowess when he'd climbed onto a table to get their attention. His exact words came back to him. "I'm half horse, half alligator, and part snapping turtle. I can ride lightning, tame the whirlwind. I wrestle bears for a frolic and fight panthers with my bare hands for exercise."

Bowie arched an eyebrow. "If you ask me, you're just plain lucky."

"Thank the Almighty! But one of these days my luck is

bound to run out. Until then, I reckon I'll go on doing what I do best. Raising Cain.''

"Think you ever will go into politics?"

"I might. I'm as lazy as the next coon. And who wouldn't like to get paid for sitting around on their backside doing nothing?'' Davy paused to listen. The din of conflict had risen to a feverish pitch. By the sounds of things, the Karankawas and cannibals were slaughtering one another with crazed abandon. Pursuit was unlikely.

"My days of dealing in Black Ivory are over,'' Bowie said. "I plan to dabble in land speculation next. Maybe visit Texas, as you suggested.''

"You won't regret it if you do. Count on me showing up eventually. We'll get together and reminisce about the good old days.''

"You call what we've been through 'good old days'?''

"Any day I'm not pushing up clover is just dandy in my book.''

Flavius Harris was startled when loud laughter rang out. He glanced in amazement from the Irishman to Bowie and back again. *What a pair!* he reflected. *Fearless as could be. Between the two of them, they could probably lick an army!*

On into the swamp they hastened, two legends in the making.

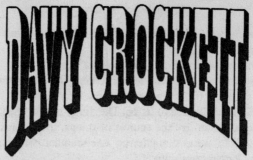

HOMECOMING

DAVID THOMPSON

Davy Crockett lives for adventure. With a faithful friend at his side and a trusty long rifle in his hand, the fearless frontiersman sets out for the Great Lakes territories. But the region surrounding the majestic inland seas is full of Indians both peaceful and bloodthirsty. And when the brave pioneer saves a Chippewa maiden from warriors of a rival tribe, his travels become a deadly struggle to save his scalp. If Crockett can't defeat his fierce foes, the only remains he'll leave will be his legend and his coonskin cap.

___4112-X $3.99 US/$4.99 CAN

Dorchester Publishing Co., Inc.
P.O. Box 6640
Wayne, PA 19087-8640

Please add $1.75 for shipping and handling for the first book and $.50 for each book thereafter. NY, NYC, and PA residents, please add appropriate sales tax. No cash, stamps, or C.O.D.s. All orders shipped within 6 weeks via postal service book rate. Canadian orders require $2.00 extra postage and must be paid in U.S. dollars through a U.S. banking facility.

Name_____
Address_____
City_____State_____Zip_____
I have enclosed $_____ in payment for the checked book(s).
Payment <u>must</u> accompany all orders. ❏ Please send a free catalog.

BLOOD HUNT

David Thompson

With only his oldest friend and his trusty long rifle for company, Davy Crockett explores the wild frontier looking for adventure, and has the strength and cunning to face any enemy. But even he may have met his match when he gets caught between two warring tribes on one side and a dangerous band of white men on the other—all of them willing to die—and kill—for a group of stolen women. It is up to Crockett to save the women, his friend and his own hide if he wants to live to explore another day.

_4229-0 $3.99 US/$4.99 CAN

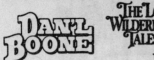

KIT CARSON

KEELBOAT CARNAGE
DOUG HAWKINS

The untamed frontier is filled with dangers of all kinds—both natural and man-made—dangers that only the bravest can survive. And so far Kit Carson has survived them all. But when he sets out north along the Missouri River he has no idea what lies ahead. He can't know that the Blackfeet are out to turn the river red with blood. And when he hitches a ride on a riverboat, he can't know that keelboat pirates are waiting just around the bend!

___4411-0 $3.99 US/$4.99 CAN